ANOMALY

Gaelan Steele
Boone Jarvis
Ashley Ryan
Kira Rosenlind
Grace Rosing
Joey Boyle
Reina Knowles
Sarah Batanian
Izzy Boyle
Emma Beck
Bryce Danosky

ISBN-13: 978-1514785973   ISBN-10: 1514785978

Prologue
Reina Knowles

A tall man walked into the vacant room. His dark hair was slicked back and his features were distinctive. He surveyed the scene where a catastrophe was yet to become. If only he had known what would truly happen, he would not have done the things he did. The things that would soon alter the course of human history. If only…

Another Place, Another Way

Boone Jarvis and Gaelan Steele

Jack

My name is Jack. I'm 13 years old, and live in a house with a grassy hill. Generally, my life isn't that interesting. That was before I forgot my homework. Yes, you read that right. Forgetting my homework changed my life forever. Let me explain.

I was going to school. My friend Matt had just gotten onto the bus. He asked me, "Did you forget your homework?" He was just teasing me. I had forgotten my homework once. *Once.* That was in second grade, but to this day he was still teasing me about it. "No!" I replied. "I didn't forget my homework yesterday, I didn't forget my homework the day before, I didn't forget it today, and I won't forget it tomorrow."

"Will you forget it the day after tomorrow?" he replied.

"Seriously?" I replied.

"Wait a second…" I said.

"Did you forget your homework?" he replied.

"Umm… I think… well, I guess technically I did."

"In other words, you did."

5

"Yeah."

"*You forgot your homework!?!?!*" Matt almost shouted.

"You don't have to rub it in! That assignment was worth a quarter of my grade!"

The bus arrived at school. I got off the bus and ran to my locker. You see, my locker is really weird. The hall where my locker is curves around and goes to a classroom that was boarded up a long time ago because... well, nobody really knows why. There's a rumor that it was a science lab where there was this psycho teacher, and there was an explosion and the room was ruined. Anyway, the people who put the lockers in made them an inch too wide, so they had to put my locker around the corner, so nobody really ever goes by my locker. Anyway, I finally took some time to think about my homework. I had finished it just as the bus arrived, and was holding it in my hand as I ran out the door. I had put it down on the porch so I could lock the door, then forgotten to pick it up. I could practically see my homework lying on the porch in my mind's eye.

I had a B+ in science, and I desperately wanted an A. It was the end of the semester. I had had straight A's every year since first grade, and it was seeming like I was about to lose my streak because I forgot my homework. Like I had told Matt before, this homework was the difference between going up to an A and going down to a B-.

Could I pretend to be sick and turn it in tomorrow? No. Matt had seen me on the bus. The bus driver had checked me off on his list. I had had no free time for an entire week working on that project. It was absolutely perfect. I had shown it to my mom and she had said it was my best work ever.

The sound of the students chattering in the hallway faded out. Was I fainting? I reached out to grab my locker. My hand hit something hard. I thought my locker was open. I looked up. I saw a wall. My house's wall. Wait a second. I was at school. Was I hallucinating? I looked down. There was my homework. I turned around, and I saw my lawn in front of me. I must have been dreaming. I heard about people who could control their dreams once they realized they were dreaming. I should try that. I willed myself to be able to fly, and I jumped off of my porch. I fell flat on my face. Ouch. That hurt. That should have woken me up. Maybe I wasn't dreaming after all. I grabbed my homework.

The noise of the hallways started to fade back in. My vision got slightly blurry. Did I need glasses? I looked down. The floor was linoleum, except it looked like the linoleum was made of planks, almost like my porch. My front door and windows started to morph into lockers. The sky started to press down on me and turn into a ceiling. The grass started to fly up and turn into a wall behind me. I could see something that looked like a cross between a student and a squirrel run by

7

around the corner of the hall/porch. Then, suddenly, my vision became clear. I was definitely at school. The floor was made of plain flat linoleum, like normal. That student didn't look anything like a squirrel. Most importantly, I had my homework. *I had my homework!*

It was really weird, but I didn't really have time to think about it. I had two minutes, and my history class was on the other side of the school. I ran into my history class. For the entire school day, all I could think about was what just happened.

Did I just teleport? No, that's impossible. Is that impossible? I'm not dreaming. Am I dreaming? No, I wasn't. If I didn't teleport, how did I have my homework? Did I have my homework? Was I hallucinating? I should ask Matt. Should I ask Matt? He wouldn't believe me. Would he believe me? I should just forget about it. Should I forget about it?

I got home. I went up to the bathroom, and locked the door. I often took long showers right after I got home, so my parents wouldn't be suspicious. I turned the water in the shower on, and walked in. I had arrived at the conclusion that I had teleported. There was no other explanation. It was time to figure it out. *I want to go to… New York!* I looked around. Still my shower.

What was it like when I was at school? I could practically see the lockers in front of me, the boarded up science classroom, the number on my

8

locker (314), even the fire alarm right above my locker. Wait. The shower water stopped. My house's water was a bit flaky, and usually I wasn't able to get the shower to run for more than 15 minutes. Had I really been in the shower that long? I guess I had been. I reached for the shower door. My hand struck thin air. I looked to see where the shower door was. I saw… my locker. My locker? I wasn't at school. I was just trying to remember what it was like at school. Maybe this was just my imagination playing tricks on me. I should just ignore it. What was I doing when I teleported? I was trying to remember what happened to my homework. Oh! I was just imagining what it was like when I got my homework. Maybe I was really at school. I had to get out somehow. The main entrance was right by the office, so I couldn't get out that way. The back door was locked after school.

I started to hear the shower again. I felt the warm water against my skin. The walls of the hallway started to shrink down into the shower. My metal locker shrunk down into the shower head above. The litter on the floor turned into the shampoo on the floor. The door to a classroom turned into the shower door. I was back in the shower. I had just gotten it to work. Why had I ended up at school, but not in New York? What did I do differently? Also, what caused me to go back to my shower?

Anyway, I had to get working on my homework. What boring essay was my language arts teacher going to make me read this time? I looked at the first page of the packet. It was titled "The Power of Imagination." *Imagination.* Wait, that was it. *Imagination.* That was how the teleportation worked. *Imagination.* When I had teleported to my locker at school, I had imagined it much more clearly than New York. *Imagination.* I guess that meant I could only teleport to places I had been in the past, and remembered clearly. *Imagination.*

* * * * * *

Matt

I ran as fast as I could down the street, towards the school and down the hall until I reached my locker. Standing right by it was my best friend, Jack.

"Oh no, you look like you've seen a ghost. Shocky must have caught you!" Shocky was our nickname for the school bully, Stewart Shockler.

I was running because Shocky had caught me trying to put an airbag on his doorstep. If he hadn't caught me, he would have flown all the way to his roof!

"You better look out, Meat! I'm going to find you, and when I do, you're as good as dead!" yelled

Shocky. He had just walked into school, and now he was coming for me.

At least now, I would have a kind of title from the less-popular kids. Why? Because I was the only person brave enough to go after Shocky directly. Or at least I had tried, but now I would pay dearly.

"There you are!" Shocky yelled, rounding the corner.

"No, it was foolproof! How did he catch me?" I thought, though it might have passed my lips.

Shocky charged toward me. He stopped and raised a fist. *BAM!* He punched me on the cheek. That was going to leave a mark!

I turned, ready to run, but I noticed that there wasn't anywhere to go. I was facing a wall and now Shocky was probably going to kill me. I felt a sudden, hard push (probably Shocky), and I found myself falling straight towards the wall. I braced myself, ready to hit my head and become unconscious, when my stomach lurched.

Suddenly, I felt like a million bees were buzzing and vibrating inside of me. The sensation began in my hands and spread throughout my body. Then, I felt like a balloon. It was as if somebody were blowing air into me, and I was expanding more and more and more. Then, POOF, I was like a floating, fluffy cloud. I stumbled, but I was still standing. Startled, I looked around. I was in the boy's bathroom, and Shocky was nowhere to be seen.

"Wait, what?" I blurted. How had I gotten here? I had to be hallucinating after that big hit to the wall. Yes, that was it. But why was I in the bathroom?

"Whoa, how did you get here? I didn't hear the door open!" said someone who had just walked out of the stall.

"I'm hallucinating!" I announced loudly. I was unconscious, so all of these people were just figments of my imagination.

"Are you crazy or something? I'm definitely real," stated the person.

"Eehh... that's debatable." I declared, quite sure now that I was unconscious and this whole thing was just a dream. I pinched myself to be sure. I felt it. "No, that can't be right!"

"What can't be right?" the boy asked, quite confused at my odd behavior. "Did you actually think you were hallucinating? Why?"

"Uh, never mind, I have to get to class." I rushed straight to class, and there he was. Right in the front row of desks was Shocky himself. His face had very quizzical expression on it, and he muttered something under his breath.

"Hey, Meat! What just happened?" Shocky yelled after noticing me in the room.

"First off, it's Matt, *not* Meat, and as far as what just happened... well, I wasn't in here. I was in the bathroom, so how would I know what happened?" I threw back with a crooked smile.

"What?" Shocky asked, confused. He sat back in his seat.

"Welcome class. Today in physics we are going to talk about molecule density." announced Mr. Tellmore, as I called him because of his rambling habits. His real name was Mr. Telmer. He rambled on about how the density of the molecules in our body made sure we didn't pass through things like walls.

Wait a second! The bathroom is on the opposite wall from the locker bay! Could I have gone... through the wall?

"Class dismissed!" called Mr. Tellmore. Maybe he could tell me exactly what was happening.

"Mr. Tellmor... Telmer, I have a question." I said. It was time to come clean to someone. Besides, he could help.

"Ask away." he replied. Right now, he was calm, but soon he would think I was completely nuts.

13

I told him everything. When I was done, he looked at me calmly, and this is what he said: "I suppose it's quite possible. I'm sure that as a science teacher you thought I should know what this means, but I'm sorry to tell you that I don't."

"You don't think I'm crazy?" I exclaimed. I guess that if he did, he would drone on about why he thought that.

"What you are implying is something that has a little bit of magic involved, but no. I don't think you're crazy. Your nervous system does connect to the part of the brain that controls emotions. But it would take a little magic for the nerves to bio-densify your molecules." Mr. Tellmore explained with a twinkle in his eye. "Perhaps you have this special magic."

I thanked him for the info and rushed out. I had to tell Jack. He had to be the first to know about this. As a grade-A physics student, I had pieced together the situation quite fast. When I was in a critical situation or had a major emotion, my nerves set off a reaction deeper down, the atoms of my body moved quickly, as they do in a gas. When my molecules sped up, I became intangible enough to pass through walls. I explained the whole thing to Jack, but he didn't believe a word of it.

"That's crazy talk, Matt!" Jack exclaimed, "I can't believe you think that any of this is possible!"

"I swear it's true." I cried. "I'll prove it to you!" I walked over to the nearest wall and walked into it. I nearly fell over. I was on the same side of the wall as before! I was thoroughly embarrassed. I slumped to the floor and leaned back against the wall. *BAM!* My head hit the floor with an ugly sound. I opened my eyes. I was in a different room, well sort of. My torso had passed through the wall when I had slumped against it. My legs were still on the other side of the wall.

What an odd sight I must be to Jack right now! I thought, *with two legs jutting out of the wall!* I quickly stood up before I became stuck in the wall.

"No way," Jack was staring at me in shock. His mouth formed a perfect O.

"I told you!" I said, unable to resist. "My molecules are vibrating, causing me to be gas-like. Therefore, I can pass through walls."

"How come you don't go through the floor?" Jack asked. In fact, that same question had crossed my mind.

"I've been thinking about that myself, and I think I have an explanation. One's hands have the strongest and most prominent nerves. Since this wall jumping strongly connects to my nerves, my hands are the first to become gaseous. I call this gaseous transition residual electro-magnetic

15

repulsion." To go through the floor during residual electro-magnetic repulsion, my hands have to touch the floor. There are exceptions, like my head and back." I explained.

"I have another question. Are you able to bring other people with you through walls?"

"We can find out!" I eagerly replied. I had been hoping to take Jack through the wall with me.

"Really?" Jack exclaimed, "This will be so much fun!"

"I don't want to get your hopes up too much. It's pretty fun, but it's a very odd sensation, almost like you're imploding, but very slowly." I explained. If he went in thinking we would suddenly be on the other side, he would get mad at me when it did not happen like he thought it would.

"I don't care, let's just wall-jump already!" Jack was practically bouncing off the walls with excitement.

We wandered over to the nearest wall, and I felt a hand on my shoulder. Jack's hand. If he wasn't touching me when we went through the wall, something bad could happen.

I felt myself filling to the brim with excitement. Suddenly, the excitement was too much. I leaned towards the wall.

I felt like a piece of string cheese. It felt like parts of me were falling off and floating in the air around me. I heard a distant noise that sounded like a shout. There was a sudden stinging feeling on the underside of my wrist, and I realized that I was on the other side of the wall. Jack was not next to me. The shout that I heard must have been his.

I looked down at my wrist. It was covered in blood. I did not remember what had happened during the wall jump. The memory was in my mind, but it was foggy.

I left the room I was in and headed to the nearest bathroom. I washed my wrist in the sink and examined the cut.

My cut was a hexagon-shaped mark with what looked like a trident on the inside. How did such a detailed mark get on my wrist? I had never heard of a cut that was so elaborate.

It could not just be a regular cut. It almost seemed like I had been branded. I knew about the magic. There was no doubt about that. I would go find Jack and ask him what happened. I needed to make sure that he was okay.

"Matt, I have to tell you something." Jack told me, sounding concerned. "I have the ability to . . . I . . . well. . . I can . . . teleport."

Suddenly, the memory came back to me.

I leaned toward the wall and slowly began to jump through. I looked back at Jack. He had a worried look on his face. Then, just like that, POOF, he was gone. My wrist burned. I looked down and an odd, hexagonal mark appeared on it.

I gasped for air.

"It's true! The memory just came back to me. You just somehow disappeared. You were there, and then suddenly, you were gone!" I exclaimed.

"That's how I stopped something terrible from happening." Jack warned, "We can't do that again."

"But you know what we *can* do again?" I asked with a mischievous grin.

"We can prank Shocky and send him packing!" Jack replied, beaming.

"You know it!"

* * * * * *

Jack

I just told Matt about my ability to teleport, and he *believed me*. Sure, he had just discovered that he had the ability to walk through walls, which *would* probably make things like this more believable for him, but still. Even though I had disappeared right in front of his eyes, he could probably still have chalked it up to some big trick. But did he? No. He believed me.

18

I thought about his plan to prank Shocky. We had tried many times to prank Shocky, but we had never succeeded. Matt had said that this one would be perfect, undetectable. But then, so was the last one. And the one before that. Every single prank that we tried was supposed to be perfect and undetectable. But every single one had a flaw. Every single one was detected. Despite our... *imperfect* track record, I still had high hopes for this prank. In the past, neither of us was able to walk through walls or teleport. Now, we could. That's a pretty big advantage. I was very confident about this prank, but I still had a lingering worry. What if... *what if...* Shocky actually managed to catch us? Before, getting caught for trying to prank Shocky was honorable. But if he managed to discover that we had powers... He could label us as freaks. If he could get evidence of us having powers, he could probably make most of the school scared of us.

* * * * * *

Matt

"So here's the plan." I began, pulling out a pre-made map, which had the layout of Shocky's house on it. Obviously, we had attempted to go after Shocky at his house many times before, but this time was different. We could not fail with superpowers on our side.

19

"You teleport to Shocky's attic-here" I pointed to the layout. "And I'll climb up to the balcony and wall jump through the door. We'll meet up there."

* * * * *

Jack

"Friday. 4:30. My room. You can come in through the window." That was what Matt had said the day before when we started to plan the prank. We were going to meet to practice. I can't believe he completely forgot that I could teleport. Well, he didn't forget. To be fair, I'd had to come in the window the last two gazillion times we had to secretly meet, so he was probably used to it. I decided not to mention it. It would be funnier if I just appeared.

"I'm going to be at Matt's!" I yelled.

"OK! Be back at 6:30!" came the response. I went out the door and snuck behind a bush. I closed my eyes and thought about Matt's room. The blue walls, the small wooden desk, the perfectly arranged drawers (seriously, how did he do that?). I reached out, and my hand hit his desk. I was getting the hang of this!

"Wow, I can't believe I forgot you could do that. Well, I guess it's a good thing. My parents said they were going to cut down the tree by the window soon."

We discussed the plan. I was going to teleport into the attic, and he was going to go up to the attic (he said he would climb up the wall, but he changed the subject when I mentioned that the wall was almost perfectly smooth). Then, we would spray paint his door with a picture of him looking extremely dorky. Then he would think that was the evil prank. He would clean up the door, then, considering us foiled, lie down on his bed for a good night's sleep to prepare for the following day's bullying, when suddenly... *BOING!* He triggers the pressure-activated box serendipitously placed under his bed and is shot sky-high. The best part is that there is no way that he can catch us. We do the whole thing while he is at football practice.

* * * * * *

Matt

I stood behind a clean, white picket fence bordering a dainty, little yellow house. This yard did not look like what one would expect Shocky's yard to look like. *Nice,* I thought. I did not even have to climb the fence anymore. I stepped through the small wooden wall and walked closer to the side of the little yellow house.

I looked up. About fifteen feet up was a balcony overlooking the yard. A locked sliding glass door granted access to the balcony. I could see Jack's cheery face looking out from the glass. I slid my hand halfway into the wall as if it had a handhold and climbed up. It was like a magic rock wall. I reached the balcony and wall jumped the door.

"Neat trick," Jack commented. "I didn't know you could do that."

"Neither did I." I laughed, "I guess it worked. Now, let's get down to business."

I pulled out a can of spray paint and a somewhat large box. We planned to paint Shocky's bedroom with an elaborate picture of Shocky wearing a dress and looking very stupid. Shocky was supposed to think that this was the big prank and expect nothing else. The box contained a folded up device that was similar to a large mousetrap. The giant mousetrap would be set underneath Shocky's mattress and would only go off if a certain amount of pressure was applied to it. Shocky would lie down to go to sleep and WHAM! He would be launched into the wall. That was, of course, if nothing went wrong. With my wall jumping, and Jack's teleportation, nothing could go wrong.

* * * * * *

Shocky

Stewart Shockler, the school bully, sat on his bed thinking. *Who was this chump, Matt?* I thought he was just some physics nerd that I was beating up and bothering, just like I do everyone else. Then, I saw the nerd disappear right before my eyes. I cornered him, and he started falling towards the wall. Then, I blinked. I had looked at the same spot and Matt was gone. I talked to Matt later in the day, and he had responded with some unintelligible gibberish. Now, here I was, totally confused and concerned that I was delusional. I jerked up as I heard a sound. I had definitely heard a sound. It might have been mumbling from the attic. Nobody went into the attic. What was going on in there? I stood up, went into the hallway, and wandered toward the stairs that led up to the attic. The stairs seemed menacing, as though it was scary to go to the attic. Up I went, until I reached a door. My fingers met the doorknob.

* * * * * *

Matt

Jack and I had everything ready, and we planned to spray paint and set up once Shocky left for football practice in fifteen minutes.

"Oh. . . dang it." I mumbled as I heard a doorknob twist.

The door creaked open, and Shocky burst into the room.

23

"How did you get in here, oh wait. . . I DON'T CARE! I'm going to kill you!" Shocky roared.

He sprinted toward me. By this point, Jack had "disappeared." I ran toward the nearest wall. To a normal person, that seemed like an idea that only an idiot would come up with, but to me, it was an escape plan. Then, Shocky caught my arm. I wall jumped. I still felt a hand on my arm. That was weird. I turned. There was Shocky. Uh . . . sort of. There was at least half of him. No, that wasn't the plan. Shocky was stuck in the wall! How would that affect me? This was not good. However, technically, it also wasn't my fault.

"What did you do?" Shocky squeaked. He was quite a spectacle to see.

"Nothing. You grabbed me, and you got yourself stuck." I responded. Shocky looked shocked.

"How did I get in the wall?" Shocky bellowed.

"I put you in there. You are a bully, and you deserve to know the error in your ways."

"The error in my ways? That's so cheesy, you nerd! I can get myself out of this wall!" Shocky answered.

"I don't think you can, unless you can electromagnetically propel your molecule bindings." I responded matter-of-factly. "I have that ability."

"What does that even mean?" Shocky asked.

I guess that was too far above his IQ level for him to understand.

"It means that I turned the part of your body that's in the wall into a gas. Only I can pull you out of the wall while still turning you back into your normal, solid self." I replied, and Shocky could not respond to that. "You've made fun of me and beat me up since third grade, and now we are in eighth grade. It is time for this bullying to end! You need to stop bullying all of your victims!"

"I. . . I'm sorry for everything. I guess I don't even know why I did it. I just thought I was better than you because, well, I don't know why. I'm sorry." Shocky said in a truly heartfelt tone.

A single tear dripped down his cheek. I nodded and grabbed hold of his arm. I pulled him through the wall.

"I'm sorry about putting you in the wall, Shock. . . Stewart."

It felt odd to call the evil overlord, Shocky, by his real name, Stewart. Stewart. Stewart. Yep, it still felt weird. I guess I would just have to get used to it. Stewart. A new, reformed Shocky. Stewart.

******

Jack

I went to my 6th period Science class with Mr. Tellmore. He was rambling about wormholes. We don't have proof that they exist, but he thinks it is very likely. Matt suggests that I mention my power to Mr. Tellmore. After class, I walk up to him. "I think I have the power to teleport. Matt told me I should tell you. Come to think of it, this was probably a bad idea. You probably think I'm crazy now."

"Actually, I don't. Come with me." He brings me to the teacher parking lot. He stops at a car, and says "Get in. I'm a member of a group within the government that studies cases like these."

"What do you call yourselves?

"The Age—I mean, that's classified."

"Oh, sorry, I just realized I have to go to piano practice today." That's a lie. There's no way I'm going to have scientists poke and prod at me.

"No, you are getting in the car."

"Do you have a warrant for my arrest?"

"That doesn't matter. Get in the car."

"If you don't have a warrant for my arrest, then this is a kidnapping. More specifically, this is a failed kidnapping."

26

I close my eyes and think of home. I hear his voice getting farther away: "What do you… noooooo!" I reached out… and my hand hit my bed. I was in my room. That was close. I needed to be more careful.

* * * * * *

Matt

It was Monday. I was going back to school, and I possibly had a new friend, Stewart Shockler. I rushed to my physics class, which I had with Stewart. I plopped down into the seat next to him. A few students looked over at me like I was insane. Four other students looked and started to laugh, and they couldn't stop. The laughter was contagious, and soon the whole class was doubling over with the infectious laughing illness. Mr. Tellmore walked over to my desk and loomed over me, casting a shadow over my desk and the three desks behind me with his tall figure. He placed a bright pink detention slip in front of me.

"Why me? I'm not laughing!" I exclaimed.

"You're the one who started this uproar! Did you know that the word 'laughter' is from the word 'hleahtor' from Old English?" Mr. Tellmore murmured.

Even though he tried, he could not stop himself from droning on, even under his breath. I thought the detention slip was completely stupid. Since when did Mr. Tellmore give detention? Especially for a stupid reason like "causing laughter by sitting next to someone who used to bully you."

That was what I was thinking as I trudged toward the detention room with Stewart. Even though he had not received a detention slip today, he wanted to come with me since we were "friends." He said, and I quote, "I get detention almost every day, anyway. What difference does it make?"

I walked in, and the door was open. Mr. Tellmore, who just happened to be the detention supervisor today (what a coincidence), waved me over and looked questioningly at Stewart. *Oh, I see now,* I thought, *he wanted me alone so he could talk to me about the power.*

"It's okay Mr. *cough* *Telmer*, Stewart knows about the . . . uh . . . wall jumping."

"That's not really what I was worried about, anyway." Mr. Tellmore glanced at Stewart, "Doesn't he give you a hard time?" implying that Stewart was my bully.

"Oh . . . yeah. We came to an understanding." I responded.

"Oh, well okay, then. Why is he here though?" Mr. Tellmore was very confused because he did not know even a little bit of what had gone down between Stewart and I.

"I guess he just wanted to come. I don't even know why I'm here. Why did you give me detention?" I asked, angered by this waste of time.

Mr. Tellmore opened his mouth to speak, but stopped, noticing Jack come in from the hallway.

"You too, Matt? How come we both got detention?"

I was about to respond, saying that I had just asked the same thing, but Mr. Tellmore stopped me. He trotted over to the door and quickly closed it.

"Matt, you were correct in thinking that I wanted to talk about your powers." Mr. Tellmore said, "I would like you to demonstrate your powers for me and do a few simple tasks to test your powers."

"Alright, then." I walked to Mr. Tellmore's desk and swiped my hand straight through his computer.

"We did not expect that," Mr. Tellmore murmured.

He grabbed a clipboard from his desk and began jotting down some notes.

"Will you please walk through that wall backwards?"

I wandered over to the wall and pushed my back toward the wall. It went right through the wall.

"Wait! Matt stop. Mr. Tellmore. . . Telmer told me he was a government agent. You don't want to be sent to a 'special place' where they can poke and prod and possibly cut you open to learn how to wall jump. Let's get out of here!" Jack grabbed Stewart and I.

I felt chills making my hair stand on end. We had teleported. Teleported. Right. In. Front. Of. Jack's. Mom!

* * * * * *

Jack

My phone's ringing. It's my mom. I think she's super worried. I pick up the phone. I'm right.

"Where are you?" she said through the phone, sounding extremely nervous.

I mouth a question at Matt. *Do I tell her?*

He shrugs. I don't think he got what I was saying.

"I was in Room 273." I respond. My detention was in Room 237. Of course, I was not in room 273 for my detention today. However, I *was* in room 273. My math class last year was there. I closed my eyes and imagined the hallway outside of the room.

She breathes a sigh of relief. "Oh, I thought you were in 237. I guess I just misheard. Where are you now?"

My hand hits the door of Room 273. "I'm in the hallway outside of 273 now."

"Oh, OK. I'll be right—wait a second! I thought... I saw you... dissap... no, that's impossible. I guess It was just a hallucination or something."

* * * * * *

Matt

I walked to school the next day and found a big, black van parked at the front of the parent drop-off line. I wondered why the van was there. When I strolled inside to my locker, I saw a tall man go into Mr. Tellmore's room. He had sunken, wrinkly skin, gray, wispy hair, and the most noticeable thing about him was that he wore a three-piece suit. It was gray. Everything about him was gray. Even his skin had a grayish tint. He was very suspicious. I leaned by Mr. Tellmore's door and tried to listen to what the gray man and Mr. Tellmore were discussing, but I only caught parts of it. Here is what I heard:

31

Mr. Tellmore: "Agent Caldwell, I am glad you're here. I found two super-kinetic anomalies that need to be taken care of immediately."

Agent Caldwell: *Mumbling* "Doctor, those kids will be at the Agency in two days' time. I assure you, they will be there." *More mumbling*

I heard footsteps coming near the door and ran back to my locker. I quickly glanced at the gray man called Agent Caldwell and noticed something disturbing that I had not noticed before today. The pin in his lapel was a hexagon. In the middle of it was something that looked like a trident. I looked down at my wrist and shivered.

I wanted to ask the man about the mark, but if I did that, he would know that I was one of those "anomalies," and he would take me away in his big, black van. What was I to do? I knew that there was only one person I could go to who would understand-Jack!

"Jack, there you are! I need to talk to you." I pulled him to the side of the hallway.

"I also need to show you something." He pulled up his sleeve and showed me his wrist.

It was the mark. It was the trident mark. I then showed him my wrist.

"There is a guy here who was talking to Mr. Tellmore. He has that mark on his pin. He must work for a company who uses that mark." I said, "Isn't that creepy? I am scared, Jack. I'm really scared. He said he was going to get us!"

"I'm scared too, Matt. We are mixed up in something big. For now, we just have to roll with it." Jack said.

I walked into physics, looked at the front desk, and decided that I couldn't just "roll with it." I grabbed Stewart, and we rushed out of the classroom.

"What are you doing?" Stewart asked.

"That man behind the desk-"I began.

"Mr. Caldwell, the substitute?" Stewart asked, confused.

"Yes, him. He is evil. He is a secret agent, and he has come to take Jack and I to his secret agency." I rambled.

"I will help you. You should go get Jack." Stewart suggested.

* * * * * *

Caldwell

Agent Gary Caldwell sat at a teacher's desk, surrounded by loud, annoying children. Why was he doing it? He was doing it for the greater good. Super humans would take over Earth if given the chance. Gary was not used to being ordered around, and he would not be told what to do by some loud, annoying children. That was why he had chosen to take care of those pesky, "super-kinetic anomalies."

"Matthew Adlin." he called across the classroom.

Taking role was the best way to identify his target.

"Uh, Mr. Caldwell, Matt is not here. He came in and then left with Shocky." a random student replied.

"Ugh. I see he wants to do this the hard way. Who is Shocky?" Gary asked.

"Uh, Stewart Shockler." the child stated.

"Thank you. You are in charge until I get back. I might be a while." Gary walked out of the room in a rush.

* * * * * *

Jack

The last thing I needed was for a possibly-evil substitute science teacher to come out of the door and walk straight at us, but that was exactly what happened. Of course. I'm not big on making assumptions, so I decided to play along until he proved that he was evil. He pulls a pair of handcuffs from his pocket. OK, never mind! He grabs my hand. I knew I could teleport away, so I just stayed there and let him hand cuff me. "Run!" I tell Stewart and Matt. They don't budge. Why'd they have to be so loyal? I close my eyes and think of the hallway, right behind Gray Caldwell. I heard the handcuffs land on the ground. I'm behind him. I jump onto his back, knocking him to the ground. I had him pinned to the ground. I breath a sigh of relief. The battle had been won.

NOPE! Somehow, he leaps up, sending me shooting through the air. I'm flying through the air, flying, flying, flying... BOOM! I hit the ground. Amazingly, I didn't break anything. When I manage to get up, I see Gary Caldwell pulling out a tazer and zapping Stewart... one time, two times, three, four, five, six, *seven!* Stewart groaned. How in the world was he still alive? Then, suddenly, I noticed something. Matt was gone. Matt is gone, probably kidnapped, and Stewart is lying on the floor, groaning. I guess I've got to take action. I run towards him, and grab him. I close my eyes, and think of a county jail cell. I had been there on a school field trip a while ago. I opened my eyes. We were in the jail cell. I let go of Gray Caldwell's hand. I figured it would take the jailors a while to realize that he wasn't supposed to be there.

The walls of the prison cell expanded into the walls of the hall. The cracks into the wall expanded into doors. The bars morphed into students. I was back at school. Mr. Caldwell was not. Whew. I was safe.

Matt dropped through the ceiling. He looked around. "Where'd he go?" he asked.

"Oh, him? He's in the county jail. I figure it will take them a while to figure out that he isn't in their record books." I said.

"Nice! Wait, what happened to him?" Matt pointed at Shocky.

"Stuart was tasered. Seven times." I said.

"We're going to have to get him to the hospital." Matt said.

* * * * * *

Matt

I began to think about the future. What would happen to me? Caldwell was taken care of, but I was still worried about Mr. Telmer. There had to be more superhumans out there. If both Jack and I had powers, the chance of others was very good. In fact, the chance of others just in my school was pretty good.

36

"Matt, what happened?" Stewart asked, "My head hurts."

"Caldwell shocked you with a taser. Apparently, you do not bode well with electricity. You have been in the hospital for three whole days. Are you okay?" I asked.

"I am for the most part. Are you saying that I got shocked?" Stewart was dumbfounded.

"Stewart, Agent Caldwell shocked you seven times in the chest," I replied.

Stewart's jaw dropped. Then, his mouth formed a little smile.

"Please, call me Shocky." I laughed at the first joke I had ever heard from Stewart Shockler, former bully, new friend.

Past Future Self

Kira Rosenlind

Holly

I was walking back home, dejected, thinking *I wish I could redo today.* I had received a poor grade on my history test. I closed my eyes just to blink, and I felt an odd sensation, like I was falling, and yet the pavement was clearly still under my feet. My eyes were unable to open. The falling sensation ceased, and was replaced by a feeling that was as if I had been thrown into a carwash. Of course, I could have been kidnapped and thrown into a carwash- I couldn't see anything- but I didn't think so.

Finally, I was able to pry my eyelids open, and I fumbled for my locket. I always had it with me and never took it off. The chain wrapped around my neck was like a long golden necklace. I rubbed the deep gouge on the face of the locket. I could never open it, but rubbing it made me calmer. I checked my phone, 7:39 a.m. I saw my friend running to the bus stop right behind me. Light peeked through the leaves, red and gold in the crisp autumn air, details I had seen just this morning or maybe just right now. Maybe I was reliving today, November 13th. But I knew it was impossible because . . . because. . . I couldn't understand why it was impossible, though I could have some fun changing time. I could be a hero and receive the

Nobel Prize, or receive the Congressional Medal of Honor. I could be famous!

I closed my eyes and concentrated, focused on going to the past. Nothing happened. No falling sensation, or being unable to open my eyes, just a large yellow bus creaking and shuddering as it lumbered into view. My locket thumped against my chest as I ran to the bus, my purple and white sneakers sinking into the mud. The mud came from the thunderstorm last night. Thunderstorms were common in the Midwest, and so wer e tornados. I lived in the middle of a town where nothing ever happened, a lot like what most people know about Kansas. At least Dorothy came from Kansas.

I climbed onto the bus. Everyone was loud and cheerful, especially my old best friend who had ditched me because I was "too crazy" as she had said. I didn't mind. People came and went, but stories always stayed. Like mythology, they had lasted for thousands of years and everyone still remembered them. I always envied people who had met Homer and Aesop. They lived during a time when everything was so much simpler. My teacher had refused to see my point on the essay test. The essay was supposed to be about how the people lived then and how hard it was instead of living an easy life now. I had done just the opposite, so I was going to rewrite the essay into something completely new and receive an A on the test in the place of my G.

39

I walked into the school with a huge smile nearly splitting my face. Although I had arrived quite early, I was one of the last people to get there. When the paper hit my desk, I readily scrawled on the page with my messy handwriting, filling up one page in less than a minute. My paper had been almost torn several times. By the time my teacher yelled, "Time's up!" I had filled five pages.

I imagined myself receiving the A+ that would send my history grade rocketing up from an eighty-six percent to ten thousand percent.

Okay, I thought, *maybe not to ten thousand percent, maybe just one hundred percent.*

My every hope and dream was crushed when I received a D-. I was so crestfallen I almost asked to have my other test score. Luckily, I was smart enough to keep my secret power to myself. Okay, I had also told my best friends, Lauren and Henry.

Lauren walked up to me, the question forming on her lips, "What did you get on your test?"

I cringed, waiting for the words, but they never came.

Instead, I asked, "Am I insane, or is today the thirteenth, again?"

"How did you know?"

I was ecstatic that someone else knew that today had already happened!

"Henry thought he was crazy, too!"

"I may have something to do with that." I tried to sound strange and mysterious, but I failed miserably.

"What did you do?" Henry almost yelled.

"I accidentally wished to go back and relive today to re-take the history test."

Henry and Lauren were stunned. "That's what you did with your magic? I can think of a thousand better ways to use the power of controlling time!" Now Henry was really yelling.

"Calm down!" Lauren was able to break up any argument.

"Hello! Are you in there? Holly! Wake up!" Henry shook me by my shoulders.

"I have been awake!" I snapped irritably.

"Okay, Holly, we need to figure out how you were able to change the time." Lauren was always the sensible one.

"I closed my eyes and concentrated." I knew it sounded unrealistic and unimpressive, but it was true.

"How about we try it, then?" Henry insisted, so I did.

I closed my eyes and concentrated. Upon opening them, I realized that it was still November 13th. Lauren and Henry took my hands. My strength was renewed.

Suddenly, I felt the same feeling I had felt before this. I felt like I had been blindfolded and shoved into a carwash. When my eyes finally opened, I could see miles of city stretching beyond the far-off horizon. I knew at once this was no ordinary city, and I definitely wasn't from around here. It

41

looked like the textbook picture of New York City in World War II.

"Holly, where are we?" Lauren asked.

"The question is, when are we?" I responded. Someone walked out of a nearby house made of bricks that reminded me of cobblestone streets. She looked at us and our clothing, and then she ran back inside. The girl reappeared with another person- a girl that looked like her, with curly brown hair and eyes as blue as the sky. The second one walked up to us, and I got the instinctive feeling that she knew we weren't from that time and more importantly, how we got there. I knew we could trust them because I knew them from somewhere. They looked slightly like my great-aunts, but that was impossible, wasn't it? There was so much that I didn't know anymore.

"What year is it?" I asked tentatively. I didn't know if I wanted to hear the answer.

"1944. We have much to discuss if you are here to fulfill your summoning." The second one said. "My name is Daisy Morrow."

I was certainly confused, now. Morrow was *my* last name. Henry and Lauren gaped in awe at my relatives.

"Wait, what summoning? Why are we here? Morrow is my last name!" I had millions of questions swarming in my head.

"We are your great-aunts, and we summoned you here because we saw you in the future. Time control runs in the family," Daisy said with a tiny smile.

"If you don't help us, you'll never be born," Rose added. "Your great grandfather is sick with a disease that is both untreatable, and incurable. You need to save him before it's a paradox, and save yourself, too."

Daisy and Rose led us inside their tiny brick house. It smelled faintly of melting candle wax as if a candle had been lit a few days ago and just the faint lingering whiff of smoke remained. I saw a painting of London and remembered that in World War II the V2 missiles were set off by Hitler and Werner Von Brown at the end of the war.

Ironically, Werner Van Brown was the one who had created the spacecraft that put Neil Armstrong on the moon after the war. Still, his V2- V standing for vengeance in German- rockets killed thirty thousand people.

"Holly," someone said.

I turned around, and Rose was standing there.

"We need you to see him, there's something wrong."

I followed her down the steps, into a small room where my grandfather, their brother, slept. He shook violently as a fit of coughing had taken over him. His frail body had become tinted with a rosy pink color.

He gave a small sneeze, and Daisy shouted, "Oh God, he's dying!" I laughed and everyone looked at me.

"He's just sick . You need medicine," I explained. "It is the middle of a war! We don't have much medicine!" Daisy exclaimed. Then, she added as an afterthought, "But you can get some."

Rose grinned, "Holly, you and I can go forward a few years and grab the medicine!"

"When should I go? Where should I go? This is New York City. I've never actually been here!" I protested.

"When you time travel, you can go anywhere, anytime. There are only a few restrictions," said Rose.

I focused on the bright shining sun, the cold wet rain and the smell of crops ready for harvest. I closed my eyes and felt a hand on my wrist and the constant tumult of being thrown into a carwash. I cracked my eyes open. Instead of seeing the regular world, I saw bright flashes of color in a tunnel, the world thrown into chaos outside. Rose was calmly drifting next to me, her brown curls streaming behind her like a banner.

"You'll get used to it after awhile," she said, seeming to enjoy the torment of thousands of images all at once. "By the way, you and I will simultaneously combust if we continue at this speed without moving through time."

"What?" I shouted back over the roar of thousands of voices.

"Close your eyes!" I heard and complied.

My eyes clamped shut for what felt like an eternity, and I kept them shut, and even when Rose screamed at me to open my eyes, I refused. They remained closed until Rose's skinny fingers pried my eyes open. We were thrown onto the ground, onto a field of mud. Rose's dress, a soft and faded yellow, was now drenched in mud, as was her curly brown hair.

"You overshot by just a little," she said, shaking out the mud. "Guess what time it is."

I concentrated and saw four numbers flash in my mind: 2115.

We walked through the field to a city. *Strange*, I thought as we came across the city. Miles of city sprawled out before us, and there were miles of fields behind us. I did not know what to expect, but I did know something. We needed to find oranges and Morrows.

"Someone else who had the power must be in this time, or else we wouldn't have been able to travel here," Rose explained. "That is how you traveled to my time, of course. I did cause your journey. Someone here with our bloodline has the locket."

"The locket? What locket?" I inquired.

She pulled out a golden locket, the exact carbon copy of mine, out of her dress pocket. Surprisingly, it had no cut marring the beautiful, smooth surface. Something must have happened. My father had given it to me after Rose had given it to him.

The city was different from my time. Everyone here wore fancy, business clothing and holographic watches. Their hair was dyed in outrageous colors, each head covered in several crazy shades. In the sky, cars were long and sleek, like limousines darting in blurs throughout the polluted, smog-filled air.

Lizzie

Lizzie walked the crowded streets of her city as she did every day on her way to the gargantuan school in downtown. Its bricks had faded from many decades of use. Except for the exterior, it was generally a wonderful school, with many updates from different years in different wings. Naturally, it was a jumble from almost every year since 2087, when the first bricks were laid. She stepped through the automatic doors, her red hair flying behind her. Most people at her school permanently dyed their hair green, blue, or orange and cut it short. Red was her natural hair color, and Lizzie Morrow was her real name. Some people even turned their skin different colors, but Lizzie had only changed her eyes to green. Her hair, skin, and eyes were naturally brown. Plus, she didn't have those crazy watches. Everyone called her Morrow. They often told her that she needed to stop living in the past. *I wish I could go to the past*, Lizzie thought.

She walked into the classroom: A17B and took her seat near the window. The computer hologram created teacher droned on and never noticed when a student jumped out the window onto the third story roof or onto the giant oak trees towering over

46

the school. Other students were too engrossed in their lessons to notice strange little Lizzie. She pushed open the window as soon as class began and crawled onto the windowsill. Gripping it with her fingers, she grazed her shoes on the roof. She dropped down onto it, kicking off her shoes and leaning her head back onto the wall. She slid down and closed her eyes.

Holly

I lead Rose downtown, where most of the human-looking people were heading. I saw a school that was surrounded in oak trees. I knew that something was calling me to the other side of the school.
"The locket!" Rose cried.
She began to run to the other side of the school. Her dress that was caked in mud had attracted a lot of unwanted attention. Many stares came from the odd-looking people on the streets. I took off after her and came to where she was watching a girl with closed eyes on the third story roof. The girl looked strikingly similar to me, with red hair, dark skin, and facial features that were nearly identical to mine. I caught a glimpse of gold around her neck- the locket. Her eyes flicked open, and even they were green, too.

Lizzie

Lizzie's eyes flicked open, and she saw two figures standing on the ground below her. One looked

almost exactly like Lizzie, and the other- the other
was Rose. She had heard stories. There were gold
glints appearing from their old-fashioned clothing.
Each of them wore a locket exactly like her own.
She stood abruptly and nearly fell off the roof.
Grabbing her shoes and slipping them back on; she
grabbed onto a nearby branch and leapt from one
to the other until she reached the ground. Turning
to the strangely familiar strangers, she smiled.
"So," she said. "You came!"
"My name is Rose Morrow, and this is Holly."
Lizzie's feet hit the ground. She stared at the
strangely familiar girl, and then she realized that it
was like looking at her aunt. Actually, if this girl
was who she said she was, then Lizzie was looking
at a younger version of her aunt.

Holly

I stared back at the girl, wondering who she was
and what she was thinking about.
"My name is Rose Morrow, and this is Holly,"
Rose repeated, seeming to draw the girl out of her
thoughts.
"You really need to follow me," the girl was
smiling now.
Grabbing us by the wrists, she dragged us through
the busy streets, narrowly missing a head
clobbering. I guess the future is slightly like the
past- or in my case, the present. This time warp
was really beginning to make my head hurt.

48

Then, I noticed something, she hadn't told us her name yet, so I asked her.

"Lizzie," she shouted back without a pause. She led us like ducklings from the massive trees to a small, quaint little house that was painted bright yellow.

That's odd, I thought. *If this is the future, then why is this house so old?*

A raspy voice mumbled from a hologram on the front door. A tiny old woman hobbled around and fumbled for the door on the other side. Lizzie beat her to it and swung open the door. The old woman was short and looked very frail as if the next breeze would blow her to the ground. Her hair was a mass of white curls that went all the way down to her waist. Her eyes, full of wisdom from living many decades, were vibrant and young. They were not just wise eyes, though. Something nagged at the back of my mind. They were my eyes.

Lizzie

When Holly from the past walked farther into the room, she seemed to be amazed by Lizzie's Aunt Holly. Lizzie remembered about time paradoxes and stared at her aunt.

"You should be warned about time paradoxes," Her aunt's face grew deadly. "Holly, you need to go back alone and now! What you face will be your problem alone."

Now, she looked terrified.

"Go!"

Rose took her arm as she closed her eyes.

Lizzie's aunt Holly shouted, "Whatever you do, don't trust-"

Holly

The older me was cutoff as Rose and I left. Soon, I felt Rose let go of my arm, and I pondered what she-I had meant by 'don't trust'. I flopped to the floor of Rose and Daisy's house. Lauren approached me with cold smiles plastered on her face. I didn't see Henry anywhere.

"What is going on?"

"Subject M, " Lauren's voice sounded odd, almost mechanical. I tried to change the time and go forward, back to my present, but before I could time travel, two hands caught each of my arms. Suddenly, I found myself surrounded by bright lights and modern equipment. Lauren smirked at me.

"Alright," she said. "We can do this the easy way, or we can do this the hard way."

Ropes cut into my wrists and ankles. The chair that I was tied to was made from cold metal.

"How did you manipulate my abilities?" I demanded.

"It's easy. You're not the only driver," cackled Lauren.

Henry was nowhere to be seen. I was kind of glad; Lauren was scary enough for both of them.

"What do you want to know?" I asked cautiously.
"How did-"
I wiggled my wrists, attempting to free myself
from the bindings.
"That's not going to work," Lauren sung. "Maybe
you'll take a nap and think about what I've said."
She blew powder from a glass vial in my face.
My brain hurt, and a deep throbbing rose up in my
head. I yanked my hand free with several tugs. My
nails dug into the rope holding down my other
hand. The rope broke free- Lauren was never very
good at tying knots. I quickly unlaced the ropes
that wrapped around my legs. I almost yelped
when I heard noises coming down the hallways to
my left and right. I spied a ladder during my quick
scan of the room. Vaulting over the chair, I clung
to the ladder and began climbing rapidly. The
noises came closer and closer and closer. I could
hear voices and footsteps, and suddenly, an
outraged shriek filled the room. Two figures darted
into the room. I rose higher, not daring to take a
single breath. I was now about three stories off of
the floor. I hoped the darkness would conceal me.
Several feet above me was a hatch, a path to
freedom! My speed increased until my head was
mere inches away from the ceiling. My heart
thundered in my chest, threatening to burst. I had
always maintained a severe fear of heights. My
mind wailed and insisted that I return to the ground
immediately. Shakily, my hand went up, grazing
my locket. My mind cleared, and my hand reached

for the latch, pushing it open. The door made a loud creak. The two figures, who appeared considerably smaller now, looked up at me. They shouted at me as I pulled myself out onto the roof. The sun hit me, warming my bones. I closed my eyes and stood there feeling calm for the first time since my abilities had come to me. I had made a severe mistake trusting Lauren and Henry, though who else would I tell? Audrey. Her name came to mind, of course. I needed to get home immediately. My eyes flickered open as noises from below me came up the ladder. A highway ran beneath me, nearly two stories below where I stood. There was no way to climb down the sheer face of the warehouse. I looked the other way and saw a truck that was carrying a mattress speed toward the warehouse. If only I could figure out a way to launch myself into the back and calculate the distance so that I would not die. I was going to stop time. It was relatively the same as time travel. "Alright," I muttered, counting down. "Three . . . two . . . one!" I leapt from the roof, landing squarely on the mattress. I gasped in air because the moment of weightlessness had stolen the air from my lungs. I touched my arm, and I could see something burning my flesh. I pressed my sleeve against my left forearm to stop the bleeding. My birthmark, a trident in a hexagon began to bleed. I clenched my teeth in pain. An unfamiliar landscape surrounded me; the dense forest was nothing like the trees I knew. Still, I had to be somewhere near

52

school, which was where I had hoped to be. My eyelids felt heavy, and I leaned back against the back of the truck. I pulled my sleeve away from the mark on my left forearm.

What could this mean? I wondered. This was another thing I would have to mention to Audrey. I scanned my surroundings, catching a glimpse of both sides of the road. The road looked more and more familiar by the second. Then, I saw my school, partially hidden by the trees. Stopping time was easier now, allowing more than a few seconds as I leapt out of the truck. I looked like a mess, with my muddy clothes and my messy hair. I ran up to the school, flinging open the doors. There must be some way to let her know. I must tell Audrey about my ordeal.

"Hi Holly," Audrey greeted me in a cordial manner. Audrey was my best friend, and I knew I had made a mistake trusting Henry and Lauren, but Audrey wouldn't try to kill me. I had to make her believe my crazy story, though. I thought about paraphrasing it. I stared off into the distance and thought that I might be crazy. I hadn't realized that I had spoken aloud until she pondered,

"Why?"

"It's just that… yesterday I think I traveled back through time," I quickly tried to explain myself. She laughed at me. Of course she did, after all the tricks I had played on her.

"Holly! Do you expect me to believe such nonsense? I'm not *that* gullible!" She chuckled.

I tried to be completely sincere as I protested. "No, no! I swear I'm telling the truth!"

"Then prove it to me," Audrey retorted, crossing her arms with a faint smile on her lips.

"Ok," I disappeared from my spot, thinking of watches of the future. No, she would just assume it was a high-tech watch from today's world. I needed a watch from a long time ago, but a brand new one.

I was on target. A shop on a corner. 1853 watches lined the shop walls. I snatched several quickly. They looked almost brand new. Though the least expensive looking- I didn't want to put them in debt if I could help it- the watches looked like they would prove my point. I stashed the watches inside my green coat. I escaped just as the shop owner, a stocky little man with brown eyes and a sour look on his face, approached me. His eyes enlarged and he dropped the boxes he was carrying. I quickly went back to where Audrey was waiting.

"Holly, where'd you go?" Audrey hollered.

"Back in time," I smiled slyly and opened my coat. "And I have my proof."

Audrey's mouth hung open, "Where'd you get those?"

My smile widened, "About a hundred or so years ago and they're brand new too."

"But how is this possible?"

I shrugged, not wanting to go into a full winded explanation I just replied," I don't know, it just is."

She ever so slightly winced, "I can't believe I'm actually saying this, but I actually feel like I have to believe you now. Not to be offensive or anything."

I attempt to lighten the quickly darkening mood, " Pretty crazy though, right?"

Her only response was a soft, "Yeah."

"Oh class is starting soon!" I noticed where her line of sight was, the large clock above the stage. "See you later, now you know I'm not lying!"

My mind was lost in clouds of thought as I took a wrong turn to the abandoned science room. I turned around and finally reached the room. I paused in front of the door. Something about it seemed out of place yet familiar at the same time. A mark was engraved on the surface of the door- the one matching my own! It was more than a simple coincidence, I knew that. Something had drawn me here. Cautiously, I turned the knob and pushed it open with a loud creak. I sighed, so much for stealth. I felt blind in here, for a thick layer of dust had settled on the abandoned desks and chairs. I dragged out a chair and sat, resting my elbows on the desk. There was no particular reason for me to stay in this room. It just felt right; I could tell that something big was going to happen here. And I was in the perfect place for those like me, those with the mark. I wondered if they controlled time too or if they had other abilities. I guess I would find out soon enough.

Double Sided

Ashley Ryan

Very strange things have been happening. My mother went to cold Antarctica-millions of miles away-for research. My father had gone to Hawaii to study the blazing red lava, many, many miles away.

When I asked my sister, Rosemary, why, she said, "for more money."

I remember the day my parents left, one to the heat, and one to the cold. My mother had pushed her black hair behind her ear, and placed my orange hair behind my ear. A single tear rolled down her cheek.

My mother hugged me tightly and whispered, "I will miss you."

I nodded and wrapped my arms around my mom. My dad patted me on my head and gave me a thumbs up. He examined my pale hands quickly while Rosemary and my mom watched with looks of placid concern. Then, before they left in the yellow taxi, they exchanged a few words with Rosemary, glancing nervously at me. Then my parents left, leaving us a car and a house.

I woke up on an old leather couch shaking horribly. Mom...Dad...I started crying, tears streaming down my face and my body shaking. This was the tenth time I've had this dream ever since my parents left. I let out a possessive sigh, wiping at my eyes, my face cold from an open window. Suddenly, I hear a loud, harsh cough. Rosemary! Forgetting my dream, I jumped off the chair and raced through the door of the kitchen, where Rosemary stood, hand on a counter.

"Okay, you're going to the hospital," I ordered my 19-year-old sister, greatly worried, since she was the last family member I had alive and nearby. "No, no, I'm fine," my sister wheezed, starting into a fit of horrible coughing. I glared at my sister for a second and then twisted my head to the side. "If you just have strep throat or a little cold, I'll do the dishes for a whole week, Rosemary," I reasoned skillfully. Rosemary's eyes gleamed, and her mouth opened slowly. "Fine, Audrey. Go get in the car," Rosemary agreed, snatching her keys off the marble countertop. I skidded across the dull, dirty stone floor and raced out the door to a day of beautiful sunshine that eagerly welcomed me. I traipsed to a carved, mossy path to a dented, rusty brown car. How it still stands makes me wonder. Quickly, I faced my house, which has two rooms and has no chimney. Thankfully, it seems abandoned, so we never need to worry about unexpected visitors. I turned back to the car and gently opened the front door. I gingerly climbed in and sat myself on a bug-infested leather seat. I closed the door and leaned away from my seat, feeling small creatures crawling on my back. I took a deep breath and ignored them. Just a minute later, my sister came wobbling out, seeming to have trouble breathing. I felt tempted to hop out and help Rosemary, but all she would do is protest. I heard a bug drop onto my seat and turned, ready to swat. But when I turned, the bug was in an ice cube. I picked it up and saw it was an ant encased in solid ice.

Strange...

Rosemary finally climbed into the car with deep, wheezing breaths. "Rosemary, I found a bug encased in ice...It's like...an ice cube," I commented, shoving the frozen ant into her face. Rosemary's face turned pale and she snatched the ant from me.

"It's nothing! Now let's get to the hospital," she insisted, throwing the bug out the window.

"But..." I started.

"Let's just get to the hospital like you suggested, Audrey," Rosemary sighed, a look of concern plastered to her face. Finding an ant encased in ice is extremely rare, if even possible. Why won't Rosemary listen to me? What's so bad about it anyways? If we were to donate the ant to science, imagine the discovery that could be made! I didn't respond however.

Slowly, I turned away from Rosemary and looked out the hole where a window should be. Not long afterwards, we arrived. I hopped out of the car and started towards the tall, looming hospital with my sister. As I walked, I felt people glaring disgustedly at my sister and me, probably judging our ragged clothes, messy hair, and torn-up shoes. I felt anger course through me, my sister's hand in mine feeling oddly warm.

Then I screamed, my dark blue eyes widening, "Your sleeve is on fire!"

"Just ignore it," my sister whispers, hiding her singed brown sleeve, "it's just probably a trick of the light."

The problem though wasn't a trick of the light. I know it wasn't. But Rosemary would argue and say she is right, because she is older. Why would Rosemary hide a singed sleeve though? I would have questioned her, but with how ill she was, I left her alone, and instead brushed a lock of my fiery orange hair behind my ear.

For some reason though, whenever I go into a public place with my sister, there is always somebody shrieking about something being on fire. That is quite strange, but I just shrugged it off, gripping my sister's callous-covered hand.

We entered the hospital, Rosemary reluctantly entering, with fear hidden well in her gray eyes. She led me to the stairs and started climbing.

"We're going to use the elevator," I yelled at her, looking away from the birch-wood stairs.

"I need exercise. Come on," my sister urged, trying to seem better.

"I'll bump up my doing dishes for a month," I reasoned, climbing after my stubborn sister.

"Fine. But I can go up a single flight of stairs. I'm still strong, Audrey," Rosemary sighed exhaustedly, marching down the stairs, wheezing quietly and quickly at each step.

"I know you're still strong," I responded, leading her like a horse to the elevator.

The main reason I wished for her not to climb the stairs was because I was afraid she would just stop breathing and collapse, causing even more brain trauma then because of low oxygen. I shake my head quickly and press my thumb onto a button with a two that is colored in with rainbow colors. This is a main place for graffiti. The elevator walls are even covered in rainbows, clouds, and unicorns on swings.

The elevator suddenly jolted upward, slowing down afterwards. This hospital is ironically a great hospital, it just doesn't invest its money in the building, but that doesn't bother me, since my home isn't the most well-kept.

The elevator stopped quickly, almost throwing Rosemary to the dull, stone floor. A loud, grating noise, ringing loudly through the elevator harmed my ears, and I winced. Slowly, the doors opened, revealing a beautiful white area.

Desks were strewn about, people looking toward the computer screens. There is a constant clicking and shuffling of steps throughout the whole room.

To be honest, I've never seen so many computers, not even at school.

Rosemary guided me forward, then to the left where people sat on chairs. Every so often a nurse came to fetch one of them.

Rosemary went to a nurse and led me to a flower-decorated couch, that was a lavish purply color, pointing at the cushion.

With a small sigh, I obeyed my sister, plopping onto the couch.

I saw Rosemary talking to the nurse, her flaming hair rippling each time she nods. Nervously, I rubbed my hands on the couch.

The nurse smiled widely, throwing her brown hair back. She motioned to me to come, and I saw Rosemary's hair swaying sideways in quick movements.

On sudden impulse, I raced to Rosemary's side, grasping her hand. As soon as I took Rosemary's hand, I almost jumped back because her hand is deathly cold. It is as if she had been caught in a snowstorm, a very cold, long snowstorm.

The brunette nurse happily showed Rosemary and I to a clinic room, asking me questions an adult would ask a six-year-old, instead of talking to me like the thirteen-year-old I am. Part of me wanted to respond sarcastically, but for poor Rosemary's sake, I politely responded and quaintly smiled.

The nurse stopped at a door, knelt on the floor, and waved wildly at me.

With the most polite smile I could manage, I rushed into the clinic, dragging Rosemary behind me.

"So?" I questioned, pursing my lips.

"Got me a room easily. Said she pities us," Rosemary coughed out, avoiding eye contact with me.

"So? The doctor's coming?" I pondered aloud, trying to make eye contact without success.

"Yes, Audrey. Now be quiet, please," Rosemary snapped, her eyes turning to ice.

I nodded once again, obediently.

I stayed completely silent for the next minute. I tapped my fingers on a marble counter while Rosemary glared at me. I swiped my hand away and attempted a look of pure innocence.

The door then noiselessly opened, revealing a tall, blonde, female doctor with a clipboard in hand.

"Rosemary Laurelly?" the doctor questioned, sitting properly in her chair, wheeled out from the corner.

"Yes," Rosemary nodded, squeezing her arm tightly.

"Why have you come in today?" the doctor asked, pulling a pen out of a pocket of her pure, white uniform.

"Well, I've been coughing a lot lately," Rosemary started, letting out the tiniest cough.

"Ah. How are your parents?" she questioned.

"Fine," Rosemary retorted, timidly glaring at the doctor. Wait... The doctor, knows my parents?

How? Whoever my parents know, I know them too, and I don't know this lady.

"Good," the doctor tensely replied. "I'll just take your temperature then." The doctor then opened a drawer at the counter and lifted a thin thermometer from the top left drawer.

"Ah! No!" Rosemary screeched, smacking the thermometer from the doctor's hand and recoiled, fear glittering in her eyes.

The blonde doctor stared at Rosemary, as if Rosemary had gone insane. Rosemary probably was insane.

"Oh, uh, I mean, no thanks. I… have a fear of thermometers," Rosemary stuttered, her face turning beet red.

Worried, extremely worried, I raced to Rosemary, my right hand having an odd warmth to it.

"Are you okay, Rosemary?" I questioned. When did my brave sister, scared of nothing, develop a fear of thermometers and hospitals?

"I'm fine," Rosemary half snapped, half soothed, crawling forward to her previous position.

The doctor reluctantly stepped forward, giving me a questioning look. I shake my head, unsure about my sister. I am also scared for her.

"Well… Miss Laurelly…" the doctor nervously sighed. "I need you to stay here for at least the next twenty-four hours. I am worried about your… uh… mental state."

My right hand warmed again, except it's warmer this time. My sister, mentally insane!?! I will only believe that when pigs fly!

Before I can start on my rant, Rosemary places her hand over my mouth, and I am tempted to bite her. I do have a right to speak! But then, I refrain from my temptations of biting Rosemary. While she is here, the doctors can find out for sure which illness she has. And anyway, if she were to stay here for twenty-four hours, I will have to go to school. Instead of having her make my food, I can make my own fantastic peanut butter and jelly sandwiches. So I smiled with my eyes at Rosemary to signal that I won't snap at the doctor. She lifted her hand from me, cautiously watching me, and my hand cooled down.

"Do you have anything on hand?" the doctor asked Rosemary, tilting her head to the side.

"I just have two necklaces. But they're from my parents, so I'd like to keep them, please." Rosemary answered bravely, her hand going to her necklace. Rosemary had gotten the necklace from my parents. It was shaped like a small, blue snowflake. I think she said our dad had made it, and from time to time, I look at it. Wait… she has two necklaces? I thought she only had one. Has Rosemary been using the money our parents send to us for jewelry?

She had better not have, or I'd explode on her, like an unexpected forest fire!

Rosemary gripped my shoulder with icy fingers, and calmly glanced down at me with a brief smile. She must have seen me glare at the necklace. I stand fast, not flinching from Rosemary's grasp. The doctor stood close to Rosemary, wariness showing in her eyes. Before going out the door, the doctor gave me a suspicious stare, a snarl slightly visible.

Offended, I stomped forward and out the door, my hands feeling an icy coolness before the feeling suddenly disappeared.

Rosemary followed me out and looked me up and down with her gray eyes before attempting a subtle look away.

The offensive doctor stepped out too, putting Rosemary's hand behind her back like a police officer would do with a criminal getting handcuffed.

Had the doctor had a bit of experience of handling mental people? I briefly shook my head.

That is none of my business. What is my business is the way the doctor is treating Rosemary. Normally, a doctor would ask if the patient would like help, and then would kindly guide them to a room, without shooting someone a nasty look. But I guess she is avoiding protocol. I do find that odd though.

Off the subject now, I just need to focus on Rosemary; we both need to watch out for one another. That's what we promised the day mom and dad left. I was not breaking my promise, no matter what.

The doctor then led us through the little waiting room, where people waiting gave us curious looks and instead of going right to the elevators, the doctor led Rosemary to the left.

After a good few minutes, a large metal door with a small keypad was at the right of the door, with some of the numbers smudged away.

The doctor grabbed hold of Rosemary's two hands and caged them in her left large hand. With her right hand, the doctor punched in the numbers 5296, kicking the door open with her hip, and grasped Rosemary's hands with both of her hands and jerked her forward.

I followed, making sure Rosemary was alright, alright for the time being, anyways.

The doctor continued straight forward, the odd loudness of her heels clacking echoed down the tiled hallway, doors at each side going on and on for quite awhile.

The doctor suddenly stopped, opened a door to our left labeled "#056", tossed Rosemary in, and gave me a look that said, "In, or I'll toss you in, too."

Well, I guess the nice doctor has officially left and the mean doctor had taken over. She really is an odd doctor, though, with how she has treated Rosemary and I.

Without a word though, I stepped inside to see a padded white room with no windows, a bed and a door leading to what probably was a bathroom.

I then saw Rosemary curled in a tight ball, two feet from the bed.

Before racing to Rosemary, I took a good look at her and felt anger boiling my blood and my fingers becoming icy. How dare that doctor! Rosemary and I could sue her! We will sue that doctor! But, for the time being, I needed to get to Rosemary.

I bounded across the soft ground, and I felt as if I were bounding across a field of pillows and collapsed next to Rosemary and eased her up so she was sitting on her knees.

I hugged Rosemary tightly and heard an exasperated cough over my shoulder, but Rosemary hugged me back tighter.

An onset of anger and love for my sister rushed through my veins and just from those strong emotions, I became warmed.

Rosemary winces against my touch, which I find strange. Rosemary and I haven't fought horribly ever since mom and dad left. But I shift back and stand, so I'm not touching Rosemary.

Now, as I look at Rosemary, I see a rugged black singed area where I had hugged her. I glance down at my own clothes and see my clothes are still a purple shirt and blue jeans, still clean and somewhat like new.

"Rosemary? Why is there an odd black spot on your clothes?" I questioned, attempting a mature stature by clasping my hands in front of me and keeping my back straight.

Rosemary glanced down at her pale brown shirt, then allowed her gaze to drift up slowly to me, "You'll find out later, Audrey."

I briefly think of speaking out that I should know now, but I don't want to bother my sister who has just been accused of insanity.

"Rosemary?" I ask quietly.

"Yes, Audrey?" Rosemary sighed deeply, rubbing the palm of her hand over her face.

"You're still going to be checked for illness, right?" I quizzed, anxiously clasping my hands tighter.

Rosemary tilted her face upward with her right eyebrow lifted. "I guess." Rosemary straightened herself and began speaking with her big sister voice. "You do have to go to school tomorrow though. I bet a doctor or nurse will let you out."

"Ok," I nodded, fighting a deep urge to argue with Rosemary, and insist that I stay. Once her big sister voice has been activated, it's impossible to win an argument against Rosemary. So it's just not worth it right now.

"Thank you for not arguing, Audrey," Rosemary stated, her voice slowly transformed to her motherly big sister voice.

"You're welcome," I responded, immediately heading for the door and beginning to shake the doorknob rapidly as it makes a jangling noise. Rosemary deeply sighed, which can barely be heard over the constant jingling of the knob.

As I shook the knob tiredly, I think of what has happened. The doctor turning aggressive towards Rosemary and I. The flicker of a flame on Rosemary's sleeve. A black spot on Rosemary where I had hugged her. And most importantly, the ant completely encased in ice.

That all happened today.

I'd have to say today is the most busy, odd day I have ever experienced.

I just wish everything could be normal, well partially.

The door is suddenly jerked open, unexpectedly pushing me back, a small gasp of fear from Rosemary.

I slipped away from the door to avoid getting squished and stood in front of the doorway.

A tall, buff man with black hair, stood in the doorway, with a bright smiling face shining down at me.

My eyes widen. The bright smile on the man's face doesn't match up with the rest of him. I could easily place him in a boxing match, cuffing another guy over the head.

"Yea?" he asked, with a thick German accent.

"Um… I was thrown in here with my sister, but I didn't do anything," I gulped, feeling intimidated.

The man suspiciously looked me up and down, then glanced over to Rosemary.

The man glanced back at me, smiled and stepped out of the way, "I just need your first and last name."

"Audrey Laurelly," I answered, warming up to the trusting, kind man.

"Would you like somebody to drive you home?" he questioned, talking to me normally instead of like a six-year old, unlike the way many other nurses talk to me.

"Um..." I trailed off. I don't want anybody to see my home and the horrible condition it is... But Rosemary had to drive us here, so it would be a long walk. "I'm fine."

"Ok, have a good afternoon, Miss Audrey," the man responded, waving kindly at me before closing the door and going farther down the hallway.

With one last glance at Rosemary's door and a feeling of sorrow, I raced out of the mental institute part of the hospital and found my way out of the hospital as quickly as possible to avoid the odd angry doctor who had irrationally placed my sister and I into a mental institution.

One hour passed and another two hours had passed by the time I had reached my front door, but by then, the sky was dark and awaiting the stars to become visible.

I grabbed the handle, slightly cold from the cool evening air. Quickly I slammed the handle down and pulled the door knob towards myself.

Yet the door stayed put.

Oh! Rosemary had the keys hidden in her pocket at the hospital, that sly sister of mine. Why hadn't I remembered that before I left?!?

I placed my face in my palm and exhaled deeply, trying to extinguish my rage. My hands grew scorching hot immediately. 1… 2… 3… 4… 5… I took in another breath and sighed unhappily. It worked.

Well, at least one of the windows has a removable screen, or at least I believe so.

But… Still… Rrr…

I trudged along the dried grass at the side of my home and searched for the window with only a screen to protect the inside of my home from the outside world.

I carefully stepped in front of the screened window along the side of my home.

In the screen netting are multiple dead bugs, some with twitching legs.

Cautiously, I got up on my toes and grasped the top of the netting with my right hand and jerked the screen inwards.

There is a loud snap of plastic being torn from plaster and I immediately fell back, landing on the mid-section of my back.

The pain coursed through me, starting at my back where I made contact with the earth, and rippled out like water does when a single small raindrop plops in.

With an agonizing groan, I pushed myself up, wincing as the pain spread further and harsher.

Glancing up, I see the screen netting is no longer there, but on the ground below.

I arrogantly kicked the netting aside in silent rage. Again, my hands are warmed, like the many other times earlier today.

As the seconds prolonged themselves, my pain subsided slowly. But the anger still hadn't vanished. Today has just been horrid, my least favorite day. Well, maybe not my least favorite day, my least favorite was when mom and dad left.

Finally I returned to reality and swiftly latched my hands onto the windowsill and dug the soles of my shoes into the crevices of the wall.

I heaved myself up so I am just a few feet off the ground.

A tiny droplet of sweat dripped down my forehead and led a shiny path.

I inhaled and shakily exhaled before yanking myself up farther to the point of where I could throw myself in, with some force, of course.

Without thinking, I dauntlessly pulled myself through the rather large window and found myself sprawled out on the floor, slightly dizzy and callouses on my hand renewed.

I'm just glad I'm rather tiny for my age, I could've gotten my legs caught on the windowsill and stayed stuck for who knows how long.

Kind of how Rosemary had attempted climbing in through the day when I had been at school with the keys. When I had come home, I wasn't able to find her until I had started feeling cold and went to the windowsill. When I had found her, her torso wasn't even over the windowsill, and she had fallen asleep. How she actually got stuck, I may never know.

A small pain gripped my heart as I thought of Rosemary.

She isn't crazy, or is she? No. I've known her for thirteen years and she hasn't shown a sign of slight, moderate or severe insanity. Not that I remember of anyways. Or of anytime I've seen or heard of her, with an exclusion of today. Could my only guardian and one of my few trusted friends actually be insane?

With a faint sigh, I shrugged off my paranoid questions and toppled onto the pale green chair to the far right of the window.

I reluctantly closed my eyes, my breathing becoming more shallow as I do. With one last deep breath my head rolled to the side before I appeared in a world of infinite fears.

What feels like days later, I sleepily peeled open my eyelids and a loud drawn-out yawn slowly awakened me a little more.

I blinked rapidly as to my somewhat slow reaction of the semi-brightness of the rays leaking in through the windows throughout the house.

It's a little after sunrise, so it's probably about 6:45 am or early 7 o'clock.

A little more than a hour school will start.

Well I guess I should get ready then. I need to obey

73

Rosemary's wishes no matter how horribly I yearn to see Rosemary.

I rushed through the house, gathering my limited school supplies and my small backpack, which grew to more than half-filled after stuffing my supplies into it, and I pulled the backpack over my shoulders.

I combed my fingers through my hair, so I appear somewhat presentable, and brushed invisible dust particles off of my shoulder.

Anxiously, I peered about and caught a moderate-sized window over the kitchen sink, in the corner of my eye.

With incredible speed, I found myself rushing to the rather surprisingly clean window.

I glared into the window as if it were a mirror and shrugged my shoulders almost carelessly, despite my earlier anxieties of appearing presentable.

My hair is just one step up from being a rat's nest, but that's fixable for when I get to gym class and have a good amount of time to brush out my hair. And I'm still wearing the slightly ragged purple polo-shirt with blue jeans from yesterday. They're still good. And anyways, I am much too lethargic and bull-headed to change, especially since I need to get to school soon.

Instead of using the window as a mirror, I used the window for it's intended purpose; I looked outside. It has gotten brighter from when I first awoke, to the point of where I can see the dew glistening radiantly on the grass. It's probably at about 7:30 am now.

I probably should begin my journey to school right about now.

With a small gulp, I leave my home, making sure to have the door unlocked, so I can prevent the window situation from occurring again.

The sun shined in my face so I have to squint. Dew droplets cover the flourishing grass, so the grass shimmered beautifully. The birds sang their morning songs jovially as they swooped about, from tree to tree.

With a day as radiant as this, it would seem that it's a good, happy life and that nothing is wrong. But, no, its not such a good, happy life, and practically everything is wrong.

A foggy, cloudy day with drizzles of rain with barren dead grass would suit my mood, and life much better than this.

Shaking my head slightly, I crossed the lawn, trampling the shimmering dew, plugged my ears in a childish manner to avoid the singing of the jubilant birds and blocked my face from the glowing sun and raced to school, of which, on the way, an icy trail, slightly melted, persisted eagerly after me. How odd I thought that was, especially since it's been much warmer than usual this month. Oh well.

"Hi, Holly," I jovially greeted, with a wave of my hand hello, with a thin blue binder held at my side as I rushed towards the middle of the commons to her.

Holly is my very best friend in the world. She has fiery red hair that is very curly with green eyes. She's incredibly smart (though she may not act it) and is crazy. Well, not bad crazy, but good crazy. We both enjoy basketball very much, which was in fact the way of how we met and became friends. We were both in second grade, young little children, and we were both playing basketball. We each held a basketball and were told to pass the ball with one another. We listened well, too well perhaps, but that turned out for the better, and we threw the ball at the same exact time.

And before we knew it, the ball hit both of our faces and we fell back from the force, unconscious. Somehow, in an odd good way, we became friends easily, and not that much later on, best friends. And even stranger, we both have an odd… birthmark, I guess you can call it, on our wrists that has a hexagon with a trident in the middle. I don't think of it much, but I do try to hide it from others, and if someone does recognize it, I come up with an excellent lie, which may or may not be difficult based on the situation.

And Holly is the only person that knows of my poverty and Rosemary having to take care of me, since she is one of the very few people I can trust.

"I think I'm crazy Audrey…" Holly remarked, her green eyes staring off into the distance

"Why?" I queried, pondering what has happened to my dear friend.

"It's just that… yesterday, I think I traveled through time," Holly replied, her speech slowing.

"Holly! Do you expect me to believe such nonsense? I'm not that gullible!" I chuckled.

"No, no! I swear I'm telling the truth!" Holly promised, sounding completely sincere. But there's no way she has time traveling abilities. It's not possible.

"Then prove it to me," I retorted, crossing my arms with a faint smile. Now when she says that she can't, now her joke will be over and I will not be tricked!

"Ok," Holly plainly answered, instantly disappearing from her spot.

My eyes almost popped out of my skull as I glanced around. Has Holly been spending time learning magic tricks? But then how did she disappear into thin air like that? Where did she go? Then Holly is back to where she is with the most devilish smile. "I have my proof."

"Holly! Where'd you go?" I hollered excitedly.

"Back in time," Holly smoothly responded. Holly took her coat and opened it, to reveal a stock of antique watches that look like new.

"Where'd you get those?" I questioned, placing my hand over my agape mouth.

"About one hundred years or so ago," Holly responded with a widened smile. "And they're brand new, too."

"But how is that possible?" I pondered aloud. Can Holly actually time-travel? But, how can it be? Those watches really do look antique, and she didn't have them before she disappeared briefly, not that I know of anyway.

"I don't know, it just is," Holly shrugged, hiding the watches in her coat.

"I can't believe I'm actually saying this, but I actually feel like I have to believe you now. Not to be offensive or anything," I quickly replied, my speech slowed as I still take in all of the information.

"Pretty crazy though, right?"

"Yeah," I answered, still wondering how Holly can actually time travel.

I then glanced at the large circular clock on the wall of the stage. It's almost time to head to class, but I really need to tell Holly about yesterday, but here is not the place to discuss such matters with so many people around.

Holly followed the direction of where I'm looking and her eyes enlarged. "Oh, class is starting soon! See you later! Now you know I'm not lying!"

I said bye back and weakly smiled after Holly, wondering how time travel can be possible. I then head to my first period class, Mr. Telmer's science class, pondering how Holly can actually time travel whilst I went to class.

The day passed by quickly after that. Classes, lunch, a brief talk with Holly, and more classes. By the time school is out of session, the sky has dulled, but it's still quite bright out. At least I can go see Rosemary now. I do wonder how she is though. Hopefully her cough is better so she can return home and no more weird occurrences will happen anymore. That would be nice. I still can't wait to see Rosemary though. I'll tell her about Holly's time travel (since Rosemary and Holly know one another), and if Rosemary seems up to it, I may ask her about the second necklace and insist that she tell me why her shirt became singed after I had hugged her.

Eagerly, I raced home to drop off my backpack and make myself presentable enough for Rosemary or else she's going to find a small comb and thoroughly brush out my knotted orange hair and lick her finger to clean my face like the motherly sister she is. Time doesn't need to be wasted on that, because knowing Rosemary, she'll insist that she can't speak while cleaning me up, and knowing myself, I'll shrug her off and insist that she speak, which would waste even more time and take longer for an answer, so I need to be of her expectations. After thoroughly, and gently, brushing my hair, washing my face and changing into suitable clean clothing (a red short-sleeved blouse and almost new light blue jeans with cloud white socks and my normal blue and white shoes), I then rushed to the hospital, my heart pounding quickly all the way and a small skip added to my step, for I will soon see my big sister, Rosemary.

I am now at the hospital, in front of the desk where the nurses are stationed, tired people throughout the room. I patiently waited at the desk, tapping my fingers against the cherry wood desk, hoping a nurse would show up soon. I don't want to be standing here all day. I really want to see Rosemary. I've been waiting **forever**.

I placed my forehead against the wood counter and kept my head there. When is somebody going to come? It's taking forever for a doctor or nurse to actually come to this wood counter! I'm getting to the point where I'm not going to have a single shred of patience left.

But then I hear metal-tipped boots ramming onto the ground as they come closer to the desk, and the footsteps finally stop. "Audrey?" a familiar voice questions.

I glance up and smile immediately at the tall buff person in front of me; the guy from yesterday who had freed me from Rosemary's room. "Hi!" I exclaim with a little wave of my hand. "I was wondering if I could see my sister Rosemary."

"Oh yes! She was moved last night to a different room," he replied, his fingers drumming against his broad chin.

"Could you possibly take me to her room?" I queried, "I don't know what room she is in."

"I don't know the exact room your sister is in, but I do know the floor. I'll gladly take you," he affirmed with a gentle nod of his head.

"Thank you so much, though," I conveyed, my hands clasped together in gratefulness.

"Of course," he retorted, "I'm Henry."

I glanced up at Henry and smiled widely. He's a good person, it's a surprise he works in the crazy part of the hospital.

Then we head to the elevators.

I'm now on the fifth floor of the hospital, which has less people scurrying around but there are still a few nurses at a desk.

"Hey, I have to go, but the orange-haired lady at the desk is Arlene and she'll help you get to your sister," Henry explained before stepping back into the elevator.

"Thanks Henry!" I exclaimed gratefully, briefly waving at the tall, kind, buff man of whom I could have easily placed in a boxing match yesterday.

"Goodbye," Henry waved back at me before pressing a button and allowing the silver elevator doors to close shut. What a nice person.

Quickly, I headed to the cherry wood desk where Arlene stood, flipping through papers.

"Um, excuse me?" I quietly queried.

Arlene placed the papers down and turned her gaze to me, a smile now lighting up her face. Oh no. She's going to be one of those nurses that talk to me like a six year old instead of the mature thirteen year old I am.

"Hey, sweetie, where are your parents?" she asked with a most soothing tone. Yep, she is one of those nurses.

"I'm just trying to find my sister please," I sighed heavily, rubbing my nose with my fingers.

"What's your sister's name?" Arlene questioned, lifting a clipboard that presumedly has all patient names and their room numbers on it.

"Rosemary Laurelly," I answered.

"Oh... I'm sorry. She's in room 502," she replied with genuine sincerity.

My heart skips a beat. Why would the nurse be sorry? What happened while I was gone?

"Do you need help, hun?" she asked.

"Uh... No, no thank you," I assured her, my jaw dropped.

"Of course. If you need anything, let me know, ok?" Arlene stated, sending me a sorrowful smile.

I nodded absentmindedly and traipsed past the desk to where the rooms are.

Yet, I still ponder why Arlene had told me that she was sorry. It makes my heart pound faster just not knowing what's wrong, because surely something must be wrong if she said sorry, right? Otherwise she wouldn't have had said anything.

Along my little walk down the hall, I passed a room with a crazy man mumbling something about an agency. Odd.

My hands became slightly cooled, but they went
back to normal as soon as I spot room 502.
I rushed to the closed door but stopped for just a
second.
The door is a light wood. The handle is copper and
smudged from filthy hands grasping the handle
over a long period of time. There are small, almost
unnoticeable, dents in the door. I curled my hand
around the cold handle and hold my hand there.
I'm scared. I'm worried. I know there will be
devastating news behind this door, but I don't want
to encounter the dreadful news. Rosemary is all I
have left now, and I'm scared to lose her.
I shakily exhaled and then pushed open the door,
my heart pounding vigorously. I entered the room
without looking up and gently closed the door.
Then with the will I have left, I looked up at
Rosemary.
An oxygen tube was placed over her head and the
tubes reach to her nostrils. Her left arm was packed
with puncture sites for her IVs. There are at least
five bags on the hanger for the IVs. Her orange
hair, now paled, is spread out on the hospital's
provided blue pillow. Underneath her eyes was a
dark purple color and her gray eyes exhaustedly
stared at me. How could Rosemary get in such bad
shape overnight?
"Audrey you came," Rosemary weakly smiled, her
eyes closing for a long time and then opening again.

"Of course I came," I choked out, making sure my eyes don't moisten any more than they already have.

"Yes, I know…" Rosemary coughed harshly and inhaled deeply. "Please come closer."

I nodded and stepped closer and closer until I am at her side. I'm at the side of where she has her IVs hooked into her arm.

"It sure is wonderful to see you, Audrey," Rosemary told me, clasping her hand around my own hand. Her hand is clammy and cold against my hand, but I don't mind, as long as I get to be with my sister, I'm fine.

"Rosemary," I stated, glancing away at an attempt to make sure Rosemary doesn't see my eyes become watery and shiny. "What's wrong?"

Rosemary squeezed my hand tightly and her own eyes watered, "I was diagnosed with lung cancer last night… I'm on chemo right now, they caught it early, but we don't have the money…" Rosemary began into an awful fit of coughing. Did I just hear Rosemary correctly? Did she just say the words, "lung cancer"? How is that even possible? Why did this happen to her? Is she going to die? It just doesn't make sense. Does that mean she'll lose her beautiful, orange hair? Today is now my least favorite day of all days. This is horrible.

"C-c-cancer?" I questioned, instantly bursting into a fit of tears. I hid my face in my hands and my shoulders heaved with each sob. Rosemary instantly took ahold of me, sat me down on her bed and cradled me, whispering little words of reassurance into my ear.

I continued my sobs for many minutes, holding Rosemary's sleek hospital gown in my fists.

If only our mother and father were here, they're not extremely rich, but they have enough money to get this cancer business fixed, and my parents have insurance. Why can't they just be here and not so far away? After a while, I settle down, though my eyes are red from the tears I have just shed.

Rosemary propped herself up so she's looking me straight in the eye, her fingers trailing through my rough orange hair. "I need to tell you something, Audrey," Rosemary exhaustedly blurted.

"Uh-huh?" I mumbled, afraid that if I speak, more tears will spill, when I could spend time talking with Rosemary.

Rosemary turned her pale gray eyes, with a sickly look covering them, away, then back, and inhaled deeply. Is there more bad news? What could be even worse than this? "Uh... Ah... I don't know how to put it. Well... Audrey, you know with your little ice cube ant? And how my shirt was blackened after you hugged me?" I nodded, rubbing my fists under my eyes, my fists gathering moisture. "Well, this is going to sound unbelievable, it did for me too when I was your age, but you have the power over fire and ice."

My mouth is agape and I raised an eyebrow, not playfully, this is not the time to be playful, but curiously. "Um... Rosemary... What medication have they given you?" That must be the effects of chemo, delusions, since it is just impossible for that to happen. No human being can have any super ability, it's not possible. But, Holly can time travel and

no ordinary person can do that, and time travel is considered a power. So, could that mean, could it be possible that I too have a power? It just seems... odd. How is it that I have a power and I know someone else with a power? It just seems too coincidental, doesn't it, or is it just me?

"And, Audrey, I too have a power, as well as mother and father. I have power over ice, mother has power over ice too, and father has power over fire. You're the only person in our line of relatives to have both powers," Rosemary explained, patting my hand gently, ignoring my earlier spoken question.

My family, a long list of dead relatives have powers too? How?

"You, mother, father and I are the only ones in the family line left with the power, though," Rosemary continued, looking deep into my eyes.

"How is that even possible?" I squeaked, eyes wide."It just is. And I can prove it, despite my current condition," Rosemary claimed, coughing wickedly, reminding me of her horrible ailment, cancer. "Watch."

I gulped, then nodded, blinking away the new tears swelling at my tear ducts.

Rosemary held her palm face-up and flat, closed her eyes and smiled. A tiny, delicate snowflake then floated above her palm, delicately swaying from one side to the next from an unnoticeable wind.

Then something connected as I stared at the tiny delicate snowflake dancing above Rosemary's sickly pale palm. Her necklace, it too had a snowflake, just as delicate and detailed.

"Rosemary, your necklace!" I exclaimed, a light bulb ignited above my head.

"Yes, Audrey," Rosemary answered, clamping her fist together to make the snowflake disappear, then lifted the snowflake pendant and showed it to me, "there is one for you, too." Rosemary pulled off another necklace from around her neck and took my hand, being as gentle as she can be. Oh, that's the second necklace she had! She held my hand, so my palm faced upward and she placed the necklace in the palm of my hand. Before she let my hand free, she patted my hand gingerly. I brought my fist closer to myself and opened my hand so I see the necklace.

The pendant is a bright, fiery orange and yellow. The flames had risen high and the pendant glowed. It glowed like a fire would and looks like an actual flame would. The pendant is linked onto a pale red string, which has a glow too, but it is a much fainter glow than the pendant.

"W-what is it?" I gaped in awe, my gaze not leaving the delicately made flame.

"A necklace, but not just any necklace," Rosemary explained, blinking slowly, "Our father made it for you. And mine is made by father, too."

"But… why?"

"Father made our necklaces to protect us," Rosemary responded calmly. "They're supposed to hide us from other people so nobody knows that we have powers, and we can control our powers much easier, to the point of where you can think a happy thought and you will release ice or fire.

"Since I have power over ice, father made my pendant a snowflake, and since you were oddly feisty as a baby, mother, father and I all assumed you had power over fire, so father made you a necklace with a flame pendant. Though, I do know now that you have power over ice, too."

My thumb rubbed over the pendant. It's oddly smooth. My father made this? It's so beautiful… I didn't know my father was so skilled at art. I smiled faintly at the flame pendant, just knowing that one of my parents had worked on this necklace makes me feel warm inside, and it's not just my powers.

"Put it on," Rosemary urged, placing her necklace pendant on top of her hospital gown.

I nodded and took the necklace by the string and carefully placed the string over my head so it rested on the back of my neck. I looked down and see that the pendant is three inches below my chin, so if I were running, it wouldn't hit my nose.

"It'll help with my ice powers, too?" I queried, looking into Rosemary's thoughtful eyes.

"No, not exactly, so your ice powers will be more difficult for you to control for now. I would give you my necklace, but father made it so it works for the destined person," Rosemary claimed, coughing harshly.

"Rosemary, you don't have to talk anymore," I said, acknowledging her harsh cough.

"No, not yet, Audrey. I have something else to tell you, just one more thing," Rosemary wheezed.

"Okay," I replied my back quickly straightened.

"Remember the blonde female doctor from yesterday?" Rosemary asked. I nodded swiftly.

"Well, her name is Clementine Rhemont, or Dr. Rhemont. She was, well still is, our parent's archnemesis. She's from an agency and she knows about our powers. She wants to capture us, study us and probe us… Now that I'm ill she can only pursue her interests after you, and she knows you'd come to find me. I don't know when she's going to come, but you need to leave. I didn't inform you earlier because you needed to know everything, the necklace, the powers."

My jaw dropped at the quantity and quality of what my sister had just spoken. At least I now know why the doctor had asked about my parents. I shook my head as I attempted to gather everything else. So, an agent disguised as a doctor wants to study me and make me into a guinea pig? No way is that going to happen! I'm not going to just run

off, though! I'm not some coward! Rosemary
needs me, and I need her! Some curious doctor
isn't going to scare me! Despite how sick
Rosemary is, I will disobey her and stay right here,
in this room! I mean, I have powers, so I can just
fight off Dr. Rhemont easily! "No," I answered,
"I'm staying here, with you."
Rosemary got into a terrible coughing fit and I
winced uneasily. "Audrey, if you know what's
good for you, go run home. I can't stand the
thought of dying when I know Dr. Rhemont has
you to poke at. Please, Audrey!"
"No," I responded, even before I could process
everything, before I can think of what I should say
and not what I want to say.
"Audrey… please…" Rosemary cried, inhaling
deeply. "You don't understand how bad it is to be
caught by an agent! That's how Uncle Milton died,
that's why we never got to see his body and why
we were never able to put him to rest in a coffin
and into the earth. Audrey, you're just much too
young to die!"
"As are you."
"You're younger than me! And if we got a lot of
mom and dad's money I could easily be cured!
Please, Audrey!" Rosemary howled mournfully,
putting her face into the palms of her hands, a
cough escaping between her sobs.
My heart felt as if it's being squeezed tightly. I bit
my lip and allowed my head to hang low. I finally
have stopped to think.

I don't want to trouble Rosemary, even though I already sort of have... She seems devastated by the fact that Dr. Rhemont could capture me and Rosemary doesn't deserve that fear, not one bit. Especially since she is ill, much more ill than I have ever been. No matter my deep desire to stay, I guess I have to leave. "I'm sorry, Rosemary. I'll leave. It's difficult seeing you so devastated." "Thank you Audrey, thank you so much," Rosemary weakly exclaimed, her eyelids drooping drowsily, "but come here and say goodbye to me first, please."

I bobbed my head, moisture gathered at my eyes. My lip quivered and I wrapped my arms around Rosemary, careful to not knock her IVs aside. Rosemary grabbed my head with her clammy pale hands and whispered sorrowfully, "Thank you for listening, Audrey," and she doesn't use her big sister voice or even her motherly sister voice. She grabbed my chin and kissed my forehead and hugged me tightly, coughing over my shoulder. Don't cry. Don't cry. I must not cry. Not again. "Thank you for being a good sister. I love you," I whispered back, hugging Rosemary back, just as tightly, maybe tighter. "Goodbye Rosemary." "Goodbye Audrey. I love you too," Rosemary sighed heavily before letting me go. Before I turned away, I squeezed Rosemary's cold hands once more, probably for the last time, so I remember the feeling of her clammy, cold hand

and I know that I will never forget this possible last goodbye.

I trudged sadly towards the wooden door, not wanting to leave, but I have to, so Rosemary doesn't become too worried, or so that she won't have the knowledge that I'm a captive of an agent. But, is the doctor really an agent? It's difficult to believe so, but my family and I having powers is even harder to believe but Rosemary proved it to me with a single snowflake. Yet, I still couldn't believe that **I** have powers, and that I'm the only one in my whole line of relatives to have power over both fire and ice. It's just strange.

Before I reached the door, the door flew open and revealed three people standing in the doorway. There was a man and woman both dressed in black, the man wearing a dark purple tie, and the woman dressed in a formal skirt, both of them having brunette hair and pine green eyes.

Then the next person, she was too recognizable. Her hair was a light, light blonde and she wore a medical lab coat. But right then was when I first realized her eyes, hazel and feral, hunger lighting up her eyes. Dr. Rhemont. Who are the other two people then? They don't look like doctors.

"Social services," Dr. Rhemont roared with a light chuckle, "this girl here is living alone ever since her sister has been admitted to the hospital. And guess what, her parents are far from here."

"Thank you, Clementine, and you said you wanted to adopt the girl?" the brunette woman questioned, looking me up and down.

Social services!?! Dr. Rhemont wants to adopt me? Wait… Does the doctor only want to adopt me so then I'll become her guinea pig? Otherwise it wouldn't make sense.

She probably thinks she's so strong that she can take me without a fight, but no! There is no way that I will allow her to adopt me! There's no way that I'd allow Dr. Rhemont to catch me and allow Rosemary to worry about me.

Both the man and woman slowly traipsed towards me, smiling kindly and brightly at me. They think that they'd be helping me by sending me to live with Dr. Rhemont. But how wrong are they. If they even dared to touch me, they'd regret ever being in the same presence as me again. Since that I then knew about my powers, I could use them to my advantage, maybe even my difficult to control ice power.

My left hand warmed on my command and my right hand cooled as my anger boiled. I don't have time to try out my powers right now, but I guess this will be my time to experiment.

"We just want to help you," the woman soothed, reaching out her hand to take me by the back.

"No…" Rosemary weakly cries aloud with a trembling voice.

My right hand began to tremble and became the coldest my hand had ever been.

Dr. Rhemont stepped back as soon as she noticed my hands trembling wildly. She didn't even alert the man and woman trying to get me. How cruel of her. What a coward she was, at least she was smart enough to know to back off.

The woman then touched my back, softly, but that was all I needed to explode.

Solid ice shot from my hand and impaled the door, a few inches to the left of Dr. Rhemont's head.

"Clementine, I thought you said this was going to be an easy job! She's some ice freak!" the man screeched, bolting to the door in complete terror.

"I'm not some ice freak, I'm some ice **and** fire freak!" I exclaimed, a flame hovering above my left hand before disappearing moments later. The woman screeched, following after the man in complete terror as well.

An orange, bright, fiery flame erupted again from my hand and flickered angrily above my palm. But Dr. Rhemont didn't flinch, she didn't even blink. She just smirked at me. And that was when I got fired up.

"Leave my family alone!" I screeched, my flame becoming angrier. "And I won't hurt you!"

"Try me," Dr. Rhemont chuckled, sneering evilly at me.

I inhaled deeply, my anger and rage trapped inside a little box in the darkest corner of myself. My nostrils flared as I stood, looking at Dr. Rhemont. She laughed, just how villains on TV would, and then… and then… I allowed my flame on my own

free will to travel straight to Dr. Rhemont and I
allowed my flame to engulf her. This would be the
only way to get her to quit bothering my family, I
couldn't think of any other idea. She deserved it,
no matter how much I hated to think so.
I closed my hand to make a fist and glanced to the
direction of where I had sent my flame, expecting
to see a pile of ashes. But I didn't see a pile of
ashes. I saw a tall blonde woman with intent hazel
eyes, staring straight at me, unscathed from the fire.
How did she, Dr. Rhemont, live through that? She
wasn't even injured or singed! Do my powers have
no harm on objects? That can't be! I'd be doomed!
"Ah, Audrey, I can see your confusion. Your
powers work perfectly well," Dr. Rhemont claimed,
clasping her hands together, "it's just that I'm
using something really useful; fire-resistant lotion.
Since you can control fire, I got it, so now you
can't hurt me, I do know that you can't control
your spontaneous ice powers. How sad. If you
don't want me to hurt you, you'll come with me."
Fire-resistant lotion? Where would somebody get
something like that? How would I defeat her? I
can't control my ice powers. Hopefully today
would be my lucky day.
Dr. Rhemont took a painfully slow step towards
me. And then another step, making my heart pound
quicker than it ever had before.
I opened my fist and closed my eyes, controlling
the flame- it's color, it's size, it's heat, and as I
opened my eyes again, I allowed my pale-orange

flame to travel straight to the doctor, making sure the flame was large, but wasn't too hot. Maybe adding to the size of my flame can help me push Dr. Rhemont back, that would save me time to attempt to use my ice powers.

As soon as I had extinguished my flame, I glanced over to the doctor. She stood farther away and she seemed quite surprised.

"Oh… So you're a natural with your powers, like your father," Dr. Rhemont voiced with a shake of her head. "This is going to be much more fun than expected." With that, she ambled forward, teeth bared and gritted like a wild animal.

I held my right hand open, focusing as hard as I can to control shards of ice while blasting my flames at Dr. Rhemont and having my flames engulf her and push her back. My head ached so much from all of the concentration for my ice and fire. It hurt… so much, but it was what I had to do, to protect my family and myself.

Then Dr. Rhemont brushed past my flames with such ease that I wouldn't expect from a normal person and she cackled, "You may be a natural with your powers, but you haven't been trained, so you're **weak**, like your pitiful sister." She said those last words so maliciously, her voice smoother than honey. I shivered at the immediate coolness discharged throughout my body, hearing my flames extinguish and hiss inside of me. My sister is **not** weak.

Dr. Rhemont strolled confidently to me, put a hand on my shoulder and sent me a look that said, *You might as well surrender. It's clear you lost, and that I won.*

I looked behind me to see Rosemary looking my way, her once bright eyes devoid of joy, and a single tear rolled down the side of her face full of gloom.

My poor, dear sister, my big sister, my friend, she shouldn't feel sad and doesn't deserve to cry.

I shakily breathed in, my lungs taking in more cold air, making my right hand become cooled. My blood ran cold then, the picture of my sister deeply sad still fresh in my mind.

"Get your hand off of me, now," I snarled, then baring and gritting my teeth at her. My right hand shook and then I grabbed Dr. Rhemont's hand, feeling the cold rush through my hand, not on my command though, on it's own command.

"Ack!!!" Dr. Rhemont cried, pulling her hand back in pain and fear.

Dr. Rhemont held up her left hand, her eyes wide and her mouth agape. Her left hand was encased in solid ice, not too big of an ice cube, but enough ice to cover her whole hand.

"Wha-what did you do to my hand?!?" Dr. Rhemont shrieked, smacking her left hand on a sink and counter stationed to her left, trying to crack the ice to get free. What **had** I done?

"I froze it," I responded so matter-of-factly, sending a smirk her way.

"Well fix it child!" she snapped anxiously.

"I'm not some idiot!" I hissed, showing my flame to scare. "I'm not going to let you take me!"

"You will fix it," Dr. Rhemont hissed, narrowing her eyes at me, "or I'll switch your sister's medication with antidepressants, and take you. I can easily get this ice off of my hand on my own." Dr. Rhemont raised her hand, and slapped me, and I instantly heard a loud slap sound.

I reached up to the side of my face. My face felt warm and red and hurt so much. How dare she insult me in such a manner! First threatening to switch my sister's medication and saying that she'll take me, but then she had smacked me! How dare she!

A horrible, all too well known chill spread throughout me and the ice unleashed itself again. Dr. Rhemont yelped and I heard footsteps scattering away, the door being opened and more pitter-patter of feet down the hallway.

I opened my eyes and looked at my hand, and saw three solid sharp spikes of ice floating above my hand. I clamped my hand shut and the ice disappeared.

Was it that easy? Had I actually defeated her? Had I just defeated the person my parents had fled from to keep themselves, my sister and I safe? Well at least she's not an issue anymore. Though what will happen to Rosemary? We don't have enough money together, but with my parent's money with ours, we'd have enough money for Rosemary's treatment. I don't know if they can send enough money quickly enough or if they can get here soon enough. We'll all figure out something when the time comes I guess.

Before I could twirl around to face Rosemary, I heard a group of footsteps rushing to the room Rosemary and I are in.

Had Dr. Rhemont fetched recruits? I hoped not, maybe they were heading to a room nearby.

The door let out a shrill shriek and my chest tightened. I don't even look up, the fear just petrified me into looking down and standing at the edge of the hospital bed.

As the door squeaked even louder, I heard a very robotic like female voice speak, "Code blue! Code blue!"

Code blue? What in the worlds does code blue mean? Did it mean, "Aggressive minor that needs to be taken care of?" I hoped not.

Footsteps stampeded in, and wheels scraped the tile floor.

Wheels? What would someone bring in a hospital room that has wheels.

I looked up, still frozen in my spot and saw so many things, my mind ached from taking in all of the imagery.

I had to take everything in step by step, so my mind wouldn't ache even further than it already had.

Two familiar people I haven't seen in a long, long while rushed to me. One person was a tall red-haired man with gray eyes. Dark circles from sleep deprivation rested underneath his eyes and he had a warm aura. The other person was a woman with dark sleep deprived circles underneath her eyes too. However, she had black hair and blue eyes, was of average height and had a much colder aura around her. They both had short-sleeved shirts and wounds marked their arms, and they both wore a face of terror and ghostly paleness. Dad... and mom...

How had they known to come here? Why were they here? Did they have enough money or even insurance for Rosemary? I was just so glad they were actually here, now everything will be perfect! I could literally burst from joy!

But then I looked over by Rosemary's bed.

A group of people, five people all dressed in green nurses' outfits, were all gathered around Rosemary, two with charging paddles connected to a wheeled cart, two taking turns doing CPR, and one checking Rosemary's pulse whenever it was safe to do so. They were all moving quickly and smoothly, taking turns of doing what they assigned themselves to do.

Then, I looked right at Rosemary, and my heart twisted with agony.

Rosemary was a grayish color, her eyes were closed and her mouth was slightly open. She was still, completely still. Even her chest didn't move as I waited for her to breathe in.

Just as my jaw dropped, I felt two hands touch my back and they pulled me up to the owner's of the hands. One hand was oddly warm, my father's, while the other was strangely cold, my mother's. The warm hand reassuringly patted my shoulder, while the cold hand's owner wrapped their arm around me and hugged me gently.

It didn't help me though. It wouldn't ever help, no matter how reassuring the person. My sister, my friend, she might be... dead, however much I distaste that despicable word, that dreaded word. Again, the people in nurses' outfits went in a rotation of using the shocking paddles, giving CPR, and checking Rosemary's pulse. After repeating the rotation two more times all of the people stopped and backed off, and the nurse that had checked Rosemary's pulse gave my parent's a stare and a confirming nod.

No... No... It couldn't be! It's just impossible! Mom and dad were here, and they had money... and everything could've been fixed! Everything **should've** been fixed!

I ripped myself free from my parent's hands and rushed to the hospital bed, rested my head on top of Rosemary's stomach, and grasped her deathly cold hand and allowed the tears to flow.

There must be something, something I must be able to do! Maybe... maybe I can warm her, since she's so cold. She needs to be warmed, that can help. Maybe she got too cold from her powers. It could be.

I took in a deep breath and willed my flames to come in a form of heat more than embers.

Rosemary's skin was scorching hot where I had touched her. Please… Please work. This had to work.

For a few moments, I just stood there, heating Rosemary with the hope of bringing her from the dead. But nothing happened, she hadn't even taken in a breath of air.

Would my brilliant plan not work? That can't happen though!

I stopped my flames and began tearing up, choking on my misery.

Two hands grasped my shoulders soothingly, and then my parents hugged me. My mother was sniffling and my father cried, one of his warm tears dropping onto my hand.

All of a sudden, Rosemary's chest and stomach moved up and down slowly, and a cold snowflake poked at the tip of my nose.

"Mom? Dad? Audrey?" Rosemary weakly pondered aloud.

"Rosemary?!?" my parents and I exclaimed in unison, all of us instantly standing. It **had** worked! It was a miracle! My flames had revived Rosemary!

"What happened?" Rosemary asked, her gray eyes slightly lighting up as her gaze focused on my parents and me.

"You had… died but Audrey warmed you," my father explained, looking over to the nurses who were completely dumbfounded.

"I… died?" Rosemary questioned, then she looked at me. "Thank you, Audrey."

I nodded and smiled. "Anytime." And then we all laughed, despite the earlier, dreadful occurrence.

My parents had explained some things. They said that Dr. Rhemont was in fact their arch-nemesis, and that the reason they had left was since they had so much magic in their blood, it would've been easier for Dr. Rhemont to find us.
They said they had given Rosemary the fire necklace because they wanted to make sure that whenever my powers showed up, that Rosemary would give me the necklace.
My parents were quite astonished to find out I had power over ice too, and my father promised to get to work on making an ice necklace for me as soon as possible so I could control my ice power too.
I had then asked them how they had got here so quickly from Antarctica and Hawaii. My parents said that Rosemary had called from the hospital yesterday, and there were jets stationed nearby their posts, in case of an emergency.
My parents had also told Rosemary and I that they had good health insurance, so Rosemary could get the treatment soon. That had lightened my heart a bit. It was nice to know Rosemary could get cured soon and everything could get back to how it was before my parents had left, and everything would be perfect.

The next day at school, I had talked with Holly, and told her about everything including my powers.

After I had said bye to Holly, later in the day I found something strange. The door of the rumored radioactive classroom had a strange, recognizable symbol written on it; a hexagon with a trident inside.
I had looked down at my left wrist and had seen a hexagon with a trident inside marked on my wrist. My birthmark. I had thought that that couldn't be a coincidence, so I grasped the handle and pushed the door open.

Nightshade

Grace Rosing

Washing and folding the clothes of the rich was just another reminder of the poverty that my mother and I lived in together. My father got lucky enough to get recruited by an architect for the government. I haven't seen him since. I was four when he left, so I don't even really remember him. Sometimes, I envy other girls who still have both their parents while I never even knew my father. Now, I live alone with mother, no brothers, no sisters, no one to talk to or play with. Nothing except chores and harsh, harsh Mother. Together, we spend hours a day simply washing and mending clothing of those who are able to afford it. There is one person who I do have, but for now that can wait.

"Is this the last basket?" I called into the puny kitchen through a hole barely excusable as a window.

A few moments later, a response was yelled back, "I believe so, just finish it! The Kirkland's need it back by this afternoon!"

"Okay, Mother," I responded as I folded yet another lacy dress-shirt and laid it onto a growing pile of identical pieces of clothing. I ran my fingers along the expensive silk, longing for a life I didn't live. Foolish.

I was outside on the porch that day. The rain pattered on the over hang. I did get a little wet, but that wouldn't ever bother me. Mother was inside sewing on a wooden bench in a small living space near a wood stove. Even outside I could hear the tempting crackling fire inside it, boiling potatoes in a great metal pot. I do like the rain but I admit it is quite chilly for spring.

I continued folding, trying to ignore the wonderful smell of the wet plants just 10 feet off of the porch, but I just couldn't resist. I carefully folded the last set of dress clothing and slipped from my wood bench as quietly as I could. But, of course I happened to slip on the wet wood and knock over a pail or two.

"Wren!" Mother yelled as they clattered on the ground, making an amazing racket. I leaned to pick them up, trying not to slip again. I could hear her furious footsteps echoing through the doorway.

Her head popped outside, she was still messy from the morning. Her blonde whitening hair pulled up into a tight bun. And at that point I was caught in the act of picking the buckets back up.

"Were you trying to sneak out into the forest again?"   at this point, her voice was already woven with rage.

"No," I stuttered, "I slipped... and knocked over a bucket."

She glared at me, fire burning in her deep blue eyes. They shifted towards the basket I had been working on, and then back at me.

"Well, if you're not doing anything productive, take that basket to the Kirkland's." she clearly wasn't convinced.

I hesitated, and then nodded. I picked up the basket carefully, not knowing how to make my grand exit. I just kept watching her. I put down the buckets under the bench and grabbed my worn leather boots and pulled them over my wool socks that were full of holes.

As the stare-down was ended, and I laced the boots, Mother added, "And no going to the woods today."

"Bu-"

"You heard me."

"Why?"

She sighed, and then spoke again, "You heard about the girls in the farmhouse a bit away, right?" She paused and thought for a moment, then continued, "Their uncle… or father, caught them muttering spells and responding strangely to completely normal things."

"I'm just going to my garden!" I snapped back, too loudly. A mistake.

Shockingly she didn't say anything else, but just stared at me. A cold, hard stare. One I knew very well, actually. Don't-go-to-your-garden it screamed.

I waited before answering again, "Ok… I won't go…" I picked up the basket and walked off the porch and rounded the small wood shack that served as our house. I glanced back to see if she was following me before I stepped onto the dirt path leading back to the village, and the Kirklands' house.

Little did Mother know, my only friend lived at the Kirkland's house. Her name was Alice Kirkland.

I walked down the dirt path, well worn by carriage wheels. It could take maybe 10 minutes to get there by foot, I don't know how long by horseback. I Doubt I'll ever know, but I like walking. There's more time to notice things, but today I couldn't or I'd get the wash wet and have to take it back. I ran through the puddles, sending blobs of water in all directions. I held the basket up high near my face. The weeds swaying in my wake.

I finally go to the door of their house covered by a small roof. I knocked on her door, and soon after Mrs. Kirkland opened it.

She looked at me, then at the basket, "Oh, thank you! You finished it rather quickly this time." She exclaimed, and then smiled at me, accepting the basket, "I'll be right back with your money."

Anyone at her house was always kind to me and Mother. Except for Mr. Kirkland, but no one really ever saw him before he was off to work at his restaurant in town. The rare occasion when I do see him, he's always upset about something. The rain, the paper, an empty bottle of milk, so on.

Alice's mother returned soon and handed me a couple coins, "Now, I bet you're wondering where Alice is."

I nodded, "Yes, of course!"

"Last time, I checked, she was out back in the garden. Feel free to join her."

"Thank you!" I turned and ran around the house toward the back yard, able to ignore the drizzle. There she was, her brown hair pulled back in a tight braid, laid across her short dirty wet dress. Her forearms caked in mud. She sat in front of a big lavender bush against her house.

I ran up to her, trying to look at least half as nice as she did.

"Alice!"

She looked over, slight confusion crossing her face, then surprise, "Wren! I missed you! Uh… Do you want to help me? You're the one with a green thumb…"

I sat down next to her in the dirt, "What with?"

She pointed out a wilted patch of brown on the lavender bush.

I nodded and asked, "Anything in particular that happened to it?" while examining the leaves that were left against the frail wood source.

"I don't th-"

"Oh, wait…" I interrupted, "When you're trimming it, you shouldn't cut down into the plant this far, it damages it and it won't grow back as well as before." I looked back at her with a smug grin, she stared back in amazement. "I will never be able to understand how you're so amazing with plants…"

I laughed, "I guess I've just spent too much time with them!"

Alice and I continued to talk and run around her garden. She showed me the plants that were returning after winter that I had helped her plant last year. We also searched for some that still hadn't come back, "I bet they're just late, they'll be back soon!" she had said.

"Don't be too optimistic, you never know..."

I then unconsciously asked her if she wanted to come see my garden. The one Mother told me not to go to today. I only realized when we were already there. I decided it was too late and dragged her along down the path towards the woodlands.

Together, we searched and found the familiar deer trail that cut into a monstrous bush. The trees shielded us from the rain. As we walked, we updated each other on new things that had happened. I told her about a new dress I had gotten, sent from Father. She shared my excitement, even though she owned many similar dresses. She told me a story about how when her father had come home late from work, he had fallen asleep on the cold kitchen table. We both laughed and told more stories we had repeated for the now hundredth time.

The undergrowth shuffled in an unnoticeable breeze. I quietly wondered if there had been one earlier.

We entered a clearing, maybe a few hundred feet from the road. It was packed with low-light plants from corner to corner, little dirt pathways woven between the bushes, their leaves overflowing over it. It was impossible to walk through and keep your clothes clean. Even with that, it still managed to look nice.

Alice admired the different bushes and wild flowers that had begun to sprout.

"You can look at some of the plants and tell me if you want me to bring you some seeds sometime," I told her as I sat down to check on my own lavender bush, just ready to be harvested. I would have to bring a knife tomorrow.

"Ok! I really like these." A bush was in my line of vision. I stood and recognized the yellowy flowers of an elderberry bush next to a ditch puddling with water.

"That's elderberry, it gets really tall though..."

"Still, I really like the flowers!" She called back.

I sighed, "Ok, they do get pretty..." She smiled brightly in response and bounced away, looking at other flowering plants.

Everything seemed to be perfect except for one thing. One small thing was off. A small wire like... thing was wrapping itself around my wrist. I pulled back in shock and a snapping noise filled the clearing.

Alice looked over in surprise, "Is something wrong?"

"No, I'm fine."

She watched me, obviously not convinced. I tried to brush off the strange snapping event and reached back into the bush. Trying to ignore my fear.

Again, the same thing happened. Except what it was seemed thicker than before, on top of that it had only gotten closer. I let it wrap around my wrists, binding me to the ground. It could've been a weed. Or maybe a snake. But this wasn't a snake. What was it then?

The thought hit me immediately. Witchcraft.

I pulled my hands away, vines had wrapped around them. I struggled to pull away, before Alice could see, but of course she noticed me. The first thing she did was stare. I didn't look over because who would want to talk about such a horrific event again. Once I pulled free she came over.

She seemed to have read my mind when she said, "Do you want to go back?"

Then the thought hit me, I told Mother it would be to the Kirkland's, and then back. No stopping. She would be extremely upset and worried.

I nodded quickly, stumbling to my feet again, eyeing the brush as if it were going to come up to my face and kill me right there.

"Yes, let's go… I told Mother I wouldn't be long…"

"Oh, I'm sorry! I didn't realize. Come on!" she turned and ran shouting, "I bet you can't catch me!"

I ran after her. Forgetting yet another thing for the moment. What a fool. That's never the end.

~

Luckily, I had made it home and Mother believed me when I told her there had been an accident and they didn't want anyone to get through the path.

We sat in silence for a few moments before I asked, "Is there anything else that you need me to get started on? Or am I done for today...?" I paused again.

It took her a moment to respond again. Eventually, she did look up from mending and responded, "I think so, and I'll call you back if there is anymore." Then she looked away again, which is normal for her.

I nodded, even though she didn't see me, then I turned and walked to my room. It's not really a "room" actually; it was more of a closet-shaped extension on the house built by my Father. It has two screen windows, a small cabinet, and a bench that I use as a bed during the chilly nights.

Sometimes, Mother complained about the various plants broken pots that lined the windows inside, their small vines peaking over the rips and spilling out over the bench. They thrived on all the care and work I put into them.

At that point, I sat quietly on the bench, not knowing exactly what to do now. Normally, I would've gone out to my garden, or maybe went to run around with Alice. But now I didn't have much of a chance to go out without 'being suspected as a witch' according to Mother.

I turned and looked at the vines in the pots, but one wasn't like the others. Just one. It was yellowing, tapering into a dark brown rotten color. I took it down and put it between my knees. A bit of dirt spilled out from a crack. I brushed it away and began to get up, thinking it would do better in the sun.

Unfortunately, I am a very clumsy person. I dropped the mug and it shattered. Glass shattered spilling the leaves and dead vines all over the floor.

"Wren!?" Mother shouted instantly after, "What was that?!" Interesting...

At the time, I paused, terrified.

"I-I dropped my mug. I'll clean it up!" I shouted back.

"Ok, I have a dustpan. Come and get it."

I got up, brushed the glass off my lap, and maneuvered around the bits and went back over to her.

As I approached her, she wasn't doing... anything really. She would've been working on her mending still, but it was strange that she wasn't doing anything at this point.

"Mother?" I finally asked.

She looked back and got up and walked to the closet. A few things fell out, bits of yarn, pins, needles, so on, so forth. She grabbed a metal dust pan and brought it over to me and shoved it in my

114

direction, "Here, go clean it up before you get any 'friends' in your room for the night." Of course she had referenced to the last time I dropped one, I had mice in the closet with me for a few weeks.

She sat back down, leaving me in silence. Honestly, I've never seen Mother like this. I walked back to my room. I swept up the dirt and glass but found something unexpected. The once withered plant was well rooted in a clump of soil, and it was a vivid green. I picked it up by the dirt, waving it around in the air, almost dropping it. I finally managed to get it in another pot and took the other shards in the pan and glanced back over at the plant. It seemed to have perked up even more during the short time I had looked away.

~

Later that night, Mother and I had a short silent dinner, bread smeared with berry jam and a bit of lettuce. Afterward, I went to my room and changed into a warmer set of clothes and put together a bed on the bench.

Not long after I fell asleep under the warm blanket, I was awoken by a sudden cold draft. What felt like an ice cold hand was wrapping itself around my arms and legs, as well as binding me down to the bed. At first I thought it was a dream, but it became more and more real. The limbs slipped around my limbs, expanding slowly but constantly.

I finally opened my eyes, and at that moment I knew it wasn't a dream. A small amount of moon light shone through the screen. Water glistened suspended in air. What I was able to see was what restrained me. A thick wet vine, something that one would not expect.

I screamed, but the silence was too thick, it didn't even seem to leave my mouth. I yanked myself away from the monster trapping me. The vines snapped with what seemed like an earsplitting pop compared to my screams.

I fell off the bed. I was scared. What if Mother had heard me? Would that be good? She would see this monstrosity, and even she would report me to the police. But, what if this small damp place on the floor would be my deathbed. I would want her to come. But if I didn't die here, I would be sure to die at the stake. My body would be licked and eaten by the flames until- Something had interrupted my train of thought at that point.

The sound boomed through the room, a clicking noise, sending water droplets from the vines to the floor. Each drip making me tense just a little bit more. Every slap gradually grew louder and louder.

Finally, so finally, a cold drop of water slipped down my neck, a few more followed closely behind. At this point, I was too terrified to scream again, or even make another move.

The clicking stopped suddenly, the silence overwhelming.

116

A new sliding sound echoed through the closet now. Almost like fabric on rope.

I felt the vines crawling up my arms and slipping onto my face as well, holding me against the wall.

Everything stopped, but one thing was left to happen. There was something directly in front of me, blocking any light. I strained to make it out. I gave up and realized that I could smell it. Dead leaves and mud clouded my nose.

But suddenly I couldn't breathe. Whatever it was had reached my face. Eight twig-like legs scratching and climbing up my face.

I couldn't hold it back anymore. I screamed again, silent again. It triggered a small army of clicking. All slowly approaching me as if I were there queen.

My wrist started to burn but then all the sounds in the room faded away suddenly, as well as anything else that I had been able to notice...

~

The next morning when I woke up, the only thing left from the horrifying event last night were damp spots on the walls and the occasional dead leaf littering the ground. My wrist still burned, and when I looked down, there was a hexagonal scab over it. I stared at it for quite a while before I got to my feet.

All the plant pots had fallen from the window sill, shattered on the floor. Their contents all over the room.

117

I looked around the room in disbelief. Refusing to believe last night had happened, but everything remaining pointed toward it.

Forward and Backward

By Joey Boyle

It was a cold winter day in Denver, Colorado. Snow frosted the streets and the buildings, creating an eerie white landscape. There were no signs of life, except for a boy trudging through the knee-deep snow. This boy was Alfred Lewman, and he was coming home from a long day of school. But Alfred was not the only boy walking on the street, and soon, two teenage boys snuck up behind Alfred and threw a snowball at the back of his head. It hit Alfred's head with devastating accuracy, throwing Alfred into a tree. Alfred clutched the tree tightly, hoping it would prevent his fall, but that was not the case. Instead of bending due to the weight of Alfred, the tree shrank, forcing Alfred to fall into the snow. When Alfred dug himself out of the snow, he expected to see the middle-aged tree he had grabbed in the first place, but it was not there. As he leaned down, he saw a small sapling, no bigger than a flower right where the tree had grown before. *I must be really cold,* Alfred thought to himself. He continued trudging through the snow.

As soon as Alfred returned home, he went to his room to do an experiment. He rummaged around in his closet until he found what he was looking for, a small plant. He set the tree on his desk and slowly

put his hand around the trunk. The tree grew!
Alfred leapt back in shock, letting out a strangled
cry. He landed on his floor with a thump. Alfred
looked at his hands, which were now a pale green
color. *I must be dreaming,* he thought, but as the
night wore on, it became increasingly apparent that
he was not dreaming. Alfred's mind filled with
thoughts, evil thoughts of redemption and revenge.
"If it works on plants, it must work on other
things," he reasoned aloud, his eyes glittering with
greed. Something clicked in Alfred then, and little
did he know, the answer would be too terrible to
imagine.

The next morning, the amount of snow had
increased, and the sky had turned an ominous,
gloomy gray. The wet snow crunched beneath his
heavy boots, each step becoming harder and harder
to complete. After what seemed like an eternity,
the draconian concrete walls of the school came
into view, offering relief from the cold, wet
morning. Alfred knew that the bullies had to be
waiting for him, by his locker, but instead of
deliberately avoiding his locker, he walked right to
it. As Alfred had predicted, the two boys soon
appeared, shouting insults and laughing at him.
The first boy, Le'voan, wore a threadbare and
musty hooded coat, which had a scull printed on it.
The second boy's name was Markus, and he wore a
similar garment, but his did not have a skull on it.
Alfred let the bullies taunt him for a while,
knowing that they would eventually just shove him

against his locker. When they did, Alfred grabbed Markus' arm and held it. Markus slowly began to shrink, and his clothes began to hang, sagging over his shoulders. It only took a minute, but after a minute, all that was left was Markus' coat. Everyone in the hall stood in shocked silence for a moment, but then someone screamed, and the crowd erupted. Students ran wild through the halls, and Alfred had to escape through the emergency door. The enormity of the situation had just begun to sink in, and when it did, Alfred realized that he only had one option. He ran. Alfred ran, flying over the rocks and dodging trees. Eventually, he bolted toward the forest surrounding the school. It had just started to rain, and the ground quickly became damp and slippery. He became disoriented from the snow swirling around him, and it seeped through his jacket. Alfred knew he wouldn't be able to return home. He needed a place where he could blend in. He decided to take the bus as far away as he could from the school. Fumbling for his wallet, which contained a bus pass and about twenty-five dollars, Alfred calculated a route to the bus stop. The trek was painstakingly long, but Alfred managed to catch the five-thirty bus. As the old bus lumbered along, Alfred realized how he hadn't had anything to eat since breakfast. Promising himself he would eat when he got to his destination, Alfred closed his eyes and fell asleep. "Hey kid wake up and get off my bus!"

Alfred jolted awake and saw a very large woman in a bus driver's uniform looking back at him.

"This is the last stop, so you need to get off the bus."

Quickly apologizing, Alfred hurried off the bus and into the cold Michigan air. Before him lay the Detroit skyline enhanced by ominous gray clouds. The tall skyscrapers loomed over Alfred, and they seemed to watch his every step. Cars and people rushed by, but Alfred realized that he hadn't made any plans for beyond this stage, and he didn't know what to do. The sky was beginning to get darker, and it made the harsh and bitter chill even worse. He began to trudge along the cold sidewalk, hoping it would help him with the cold.

After seeing a department store open up ahead, Alfred looked for something that could erase his hunger. He found a package of beef jerky, but when he went to pay for it, he realized something. His wallet was gone. If Alfred hadn't been as hungry, he might have been more rational, but this was not the case. He suddenly bolted from the store. The cashier quickly followed in pursuit. People stepped out of the way when Alfred approached them, scattering the crowd. Alfred stepped onto a sidewalk, realizing that the cashier was coming for him at full speed. He put his hands out instinctively, but nothing appeared. As he looked up, he realized that he stood in a pile of neatly organized car parts, each from a different vehicle. Alfred barely had the time to take note of this however, as he needed to quickly sprint away from his pursuers. Once Alfred was sure that he wasn't being followed anymore, he slowed to a walk and casually ate the beef jerky. He realized that he had never actually had a good reason for being there. It was fear that he was running from. Fear and guilt. Suddenly, on that dismal street corner, Alfred knew what he needed to do.

The hospital room smelled heavenly of antiseptic and alcohol. That didn't disturb the boy in the waiting room, as he was not here to visit. He slowly walked to room 650B, and he entered under the aging wooden doorframe. He was only in for a few minutes, quickly reading the sign that read: Markus Smith. As he walked out of the hospital, he noticed a small plant growing in one of the flowerbeds. It seemed weak presently, but the boy knew that it would soon become strong, and this small plant was the beginning of a new life.

Jumping Time

Reina Knowles

"Yes, that will be all."

"Okay, have a good night!" said Meri, turning around and walking swiftly to the door marked "employees only". She pushed open the door and stepped into the threshold as the door swung shut wearily behind her. She pulled the strings off the bow and removed her apron. She folded up the apron and set it onto the table marked "linens", grabbed her purse and hurried out the back door. The pavement glistened, and the bright flashing lights filled up the parking lot with their cool glow. A slight breeze rustled her hair as she rummaged through her purse for her keys. Her fingers grasped the car keys and their jingles filled the silence. Grasping the plastic remote in one hand, she pressed the button twice and the headlights flashed in conformation. She opened the door and slid into the seat. She set her purse on the passenger seat and exhaled, letting go of all her built up stress and relaxing her muscles. She was exhausted. She reached her hand over to turn on the radio. She jumped as the loud music shook the car with its booming bass. Quickly, she turned the volume down and started surfing the channels. She was still shaky from the scare. She settled on some quiet jazz as she started the car in reverse…

She had been driving for about fifteen minutes on the freeway. Her choice of music was not beneficial to her driving. The smooth, quiet, jazz was lulling her into a blue trance. She felt herself dozing off and pulled herself back into reality. She felt as though her heart had skipped a beat. *It was probably the strong coffee I had today,* she thought to herself. She counted down the miles until she was five miles away. She glanced down at her gas tank and noticed it was alarmingly low. Quickly, she pulled into the nearest exit. The city had old-fashioned buildings and signs. *It was probably one of those old-fashioned towns,* she thought to herself. She pulled into the gas station and parked at the open booth. She started to get out of the car, but was greeted by a young man in a uniform. "You needn't get out of your car ma'am," the man said.

"Okay…" she said. She turned around and her jaw dropped. "M-m-my car," she stammered, staggering away from the black, glossy car that had suddenly replaced her car.

"Yes ma'am, that's quite a nice car you got. Would you like me to fill it up for you?" said the young man politely.

"Uh, yes, please." She said as the man opened the door. She slid into the seat, exhaling shakily. He gently closed the door and walked off, shouting something remotely audible to another work boy. Her heart was racing. *What just happened?* She thought as horrible ideas floated through her brain. *I must be dreaming,* she decided. She got pulled back into reality by a loud rapping on the window. She looked up quickly, startled by the loud noise. She rolled down the window and tossed a wad of cash at him. He caught it and said,

"Okay, you're good."

"Keep the change." She said as she smoothly pulled out and back onto the road.

She soon was feeling more normal now she was getting accustomed to the change. She gazed out at the long road and wondered,

"Is this real?" she looked down to see the welcoming lights emitted from her dashboard. She did a double take. What had just happened?

"This is not real." She concluded as she turned off onto that familiar road. She pulled into her driveway and parked her car. She slid the key into the lock, heard it click, and pushed the door open. She was greeted by the familiar scent of vanilla from the cupcakes she had carelessly left out from the party the night before. Exhausted, she stumbled into her room and collapsed on her bed, instantly falling asleep.

It took her a couple of minutes to recall what had happened the night before. Leaving work, the drive home, it was all a blur. The one thing she distinctly remembered was that something was wrong. She had almost… gone back in time? Impossible. She was crazy. She was really, truly, crazy. She didn't know what to do, so she did the one thing she knew to do, Google it.

"I-think-I-went-back-in-time" she muttered as she typed the words into the search bar. She sat nervously tapping her fingers as the search engine loaded the results. She clicked on the first site that popped up and skimmed the article. They stated that the person was hallucinating and questioned them about what they had consumed within the last 24 hours. She went on to the second website which pretty much said the same thing and recommended that they go to a mental hospital. Curious, she looked up the nearest mental hospital in her area. To her surprise, there was one three blocks from her house. She pulled out her phone and started to dial the numbers into her phone. She paused before pressing call and thought,

"Is this really the right thing to do?" She remembered what people had said reacting to the questions online.

"This isn't normal" she thought aloud. She took a deep breath, and pressed call.

"Brrrrrr… Brrrrrr…" the dial rung before the receiver picked up as she clenched her shaking hands.

"Hello, this is St. Adams Mental Health Hospital, what can I do for you?" said a nasally woman's voice.

"I-I would like to schedule an appointment, preferably tomorrow." She said as her voice strengthened.

"Would 2:00 P.M. work for you?" said the voice.

"Yes it would."

"And a name please?"

"Merigold Bricklin" she said. People rarely called her by her full name and now it seemed strange, almost foreign.

"Nice to meet you Ms. Bricklin, I'm Cathy Willis. I look forward to seeing you tomorrow."

"So do I," replied Meri as she prepared to hang up. The call ended with a satisfying "click". It was the next day and she was pulling into the parking lot of the clinic. She was absolutely terrified. Clinics had always scared her. She hated being poked, prodded, questioned, and probed. This was going to be a long week…
She stepped through the door and the scent hit her. The cold antiseptic smell filled her nostrils and sent a shudder down her spine. She took a deep breath, shuddered again, and started walking to the front desk.

"Hello," she said as her voice quavered in fear.

128

"And you are?" said a lady looking over her cat-eye glasses with a sharp penetrating glare.

"I-I um…" how could she have forgotten her name?

"Oh right. Merigold Bricklin" The lady looked down at her papers, frowning slightly as she shuffled through them until she froze. Her eyes went back and forth down the page and she nodded slightly. She looked up at Meri with a warm smile. It looked strangely strained, as her usual face was one of complete disgust as though someone was waving a trash can under her nose.

"Oh hello Merigold, I believe we spoke yesterday?"

"Uh, yes we did," said Meri nervously tapping her fingers on her leg.

"Why don't you take a seat and fill out this paperwork." Said the lady brandishing a clipboard in one hand and pointing to a seat with the other…

The next three days were horrific, she was constantly watched by the "monitors of the clinic" who stood around watching the patients 24/7 only letting privacy to use the restroom. They even had a monitor in each bedroom to make sure nobody had any "bad dreams" during the night. She felt as though she was in grade school again. If you weren't crazy already, this place would change that.

Currently, she was in the cafeteria, which had a strict menu that only served salad, old crusty sandwiches, and cold chicken soup with little packets of crackers. None of this sounded appetizing, so she had been living on tea and cookies for the last couple of days. It was surprising how fast one could get sick of chewy, chocolaty cookies. This arrangement would have to end soon.

The other residents kept mostly to themselves. Many of them looked absolutely normal with the exception of a few. Some people acted as though they belonged there, though.

Every day they had their appointed checkups followed by two hours of "therapy" in which a therapist put them in a scenario and asked them how they felt. How was this related to her issues? She had no idea. It seemed to make sense to them, so she didn't question it. Her "therapy" session was in thirteen minutes, and she did not want to go. In about five minutes, one of the staff would come and guide her to the therapy offices, so she had limited time. The cafeteria was always hectic around lunchtime, so she doubted anyone would notice if she just slipped away . . .

But where would I go next? She wondered as she made her way across the room, pushing through people as she went. She had no time to think about that though, it was either now or never.

She stood by the entrance to the hallway, looking casually out at the people around her. She scanned the crowd for the beady eyes of the surveillance people, and when she saw that none of them had noticed her, she slipped stealthily down the hall.

The hallway was empty and quiet, with her footsteps reverberating on the cold marble floor. To her dismay, there weren't any exits or doors out to the lobby. After a hurried search, she turned back and heard something that made her stop in her tracks. Footsteps getting louder and louder...

Adrenaline coursed through her veins and her mind was blank. Frantically, she ran to the nearest door. It was locked. She ran to the one across from it and fortunately, it was open. She scampered into the small closet as her heart skipped a beat. She whipped around and carefully, yet swiftly, closed the door, pressing her head onto the cold surface and straining her ears for any sound. Strangely enough, it was silent.

Now that there was no immediate threat, she had time to explore her surroundings. She appeared to be in a janitor's closet. It had shelves of supplies and some grimy mops propped in the corner. The room smelled strongly of bleach and lemons. She turned her attention back to the door. There was no light under it and it was cold to the touch. She reached for the smooth handle and opened it cautiously, straining her ears, listening for any noise. There was none. Creeping out on her hands and knees, she crawled out from the cupboard and felt the rough stone under her hands.

The hall had changed into a large, drafty room. There were oil lamps on the striped, wallpapered walls. The light flickered ominously, and the fireplace off to one side filled the room with its eerie glow. Despite the fire, there was no warmth in the room. A cold chill passed over her like a thousand faltering whispers. Her hair was standing on end. A shrill shriek took the place of the calm crackling of the fire. The echoes reverberated throughout the room, and her scalp prickled. She looked through the room, searching for the source of the noise. Nothing. She was beginning to feel apprehensive. Her gut feeling told her to leave, run back to the cupboard, and stay there for the rest of eternity, so she decided to stay. Carefully and cautiously, she stepped over the dusty floor, steering clear of the mouse droppings. A single spider dropped from the ceiling, moving quickly as it let out more web. She quickly sidestepped it and made her way to one of the two doors adjacent to the one she had just entered. She reached out and opened the door. It creaked ominously as she pushed it open. There was a dark hallway. She braced herself and stepped into the inky black . . .

The hallway was long and dark. There were no lamps, but there was a light at the end. All of the sudden, another shriek filled the damp, musty air. The noise was coming from around the corner. She halted as a shiver crept down her spine. She had reached a bend in the corridor and reluctantly rounded it.

She found herself gazing into another dark, frigid room that was far from empty. Many metal contraptions were lined up along one wall, some hung from the ceiling, and some towered up toward the ceiling, their metal bars gently clinking. There were two figures in the room. One was strapped into one of the chairs, quivering and whimpering, his sparse hair standing on end. Where the metal bars bound his body, his skin had shiny red burns. His gauzy sleeping gown was grayish with dirt, and there were many holes peppering the fabric.

The other man was short and stocky with a thick neck. Meri let out a small, barely audible gasp as she stood, paralyzed, peering at the scene. The man whipped around and looked toward the hall. Without thinking, she found her feet moving alarmingly fast, back into the darkness.

"Who's there?" called out a deep voice in a hoarse whisper.

She stood stock-still, taking in silent shallow breaths. If somebody found her, she would be in trouble . . .

Heavy footsteps from the second figure sounded across the room. The figure in the chair let out a gasp, his head lolling and his eyes rolling back into his head. The other paid no attention to him. With every step the man took, she took two steps backward, not daring to make a sound.

The man sniffed, and she stopped abruptly. Could he smell her? She leaned back as far as she could, suddenly aware of her heart beating fearfully in her chest. The man sniffed once more, then paused for a moment, and turned swiftly on his heel. He began to untangle a long chain with a spiky ball on the end. Without thinking, she began to run. She heard a shout, and footsteps followed behind her, but she did not stop. She ran into the previous room, knowing she had just a few seconds before her pursuer caught up to her.

Impulsively, she scrambled into the last doorway and hid behind the door. A second passed, a minute, an hour, it made no difference to her. She had no other choice, no plan of escape. She would be surprised if she got out alive.

After what felt like hours, she heard footsteps walking away from her. They were getting farther and farther, softer and softer.

Once she could not hear any more sounds, she relaxed. She let out heaving breaths that she had suppressed, and she leaned against the wall, all of her muscles shaking from the adrenaline rush. That was close.

After a couple of minutes, she had calmed herself down and was beginning to think clearly. Where was she? What had happened? What will happen? How did she get there? How did she get back? Was this real? She pinched herself. So this was real? It felt real. . .

She ran her fingers down the wood walls. The wood splintered, and she felt it pierce her finger. She quickly drew back her hand and ripped the splinter out, deliberately not looking down at her hand for she knew the sight of blood made her ill. She tugged her sleeve over her fingers and drew her hand into a fist.

She busied herself by exploring this room. It was similar to the previous room, aside from the fact that it was empty. She walked over to a swing-like contraption and gave it a nudge. The rope groaned, and the chair started to turn. She stepped

back and walked over to a low cage-like wooden
box. It looked like an animal crate. Something
glinted in the dim light, and she bent lower to see
it. It was a little iron plaque that read;

St Adams Mental Hospital
Containment Crib
Room for the Insane

Puzzled, she walked over to the swing and
examined it. It too had a plaque. The plaque read:

St. Adams Mental Hospital
Circulating Swing
Room for the Insane

Suddenly, as if someone had turned on a light, she
started to notice many plaques all around the room,
glinting at her, as if inviting her to read
them. Tranquilizing chair, electric chair, binding
rope, heated chains; hot oil bath… the list went
on. The pieces of the puzzle came together in her
head. She had to be back in time, in the mental
hospital she checked herself into. It was nighttime,
and she was in a torture chamber. She had been
avoiding the thought, but she couldn't any
longer. How did she get there? She thought back
on all the instances when she had "hallucinations."

Though the people at the clinic told her to block
out the memories, they came all too easily. There

was something irresistible about being told not to do something. You just had to do it.

Whenever she went back in time, she felt her heart skip. She was also moving fast. She was exhausted, unfocused, or panicked. She had mistaken these times as her "hallucinations," but now she knew what they really were. She knew how to do it, now she just needed to get back.

She looked around the room. Then she looked down at her hands. During the excitement of her discovery, she had barely noticed the dull throbbing of her finger. It was dripping with blood and her sleeve was saturated. A splinter must have pierced her skin. It looked like a deep one. But it hurt so much…. Was it really a splinter? Her head began to pound, and her vision began to darken. Her eyes rolled back and she fell forward onto the ground.

She woke up in an unfamiliar room. Relieved, she realized she was back in present time. Wait, that meant it had worked. She was right. She had returned forward in time. She looked around. She was in an office-like room.

She peeled herself off of the ground and brushed off her jeans. There was a desk in the center of the room and two doors. One door was unmarked; she assumed it led to the clinic. The other door had an exit sign over it; she assumed it led out to the parking lot. Although the door was right there, she felt drawn to the desk. There was a stack of important looking papers on it, and even though she knew she shouldn't be snooping, her curiosity got the best of her.

The paper on top of the stack had three columns. They were name, ability, and status. She scanned the column labeled 'names,' and to her horror, she found her name. The chart read like this.

Name: Merigold Bricklin. Ability: Time rifts. Status: Missing.

Why was she on the list and how did they know about her powers? She looked at the heading. It read:

The Agency

This worried her, so she quickly left, trying not to give the page too much thought.

Morph

Sarah Batanian

"Goodnight, Piper," Mom said as she closed the
door. I heard the door shut, and the room was now
filled with darkness, besides one small crack
beneath the door that shed a soft yellow glow. I
stared up at my ceiling as I tapped my feet against
my bed's headboard. I adjusted the covers to my
bed, so I was wrapped up rather tightly. I started to
think about my day, replaying everything I did that
day, over and over in my mind. I thought about
school, homework, food and my pets. I tend to
wonder about strange things at night, particularly
because I don't have time to ponder such strange
things during the day. I usually spent my days
thinking about school and grades, but night was my
only time to fantasize about different things. I
readjusted my blankets and rolled over to my left
side. I was just about to fall asleep peacefully when
I heard a soft scratching at the door. I tried to
ignore it and fall asleep, but the scratching resumed,
even louder.
I tiredly swung my legs over the bed and trudged to
the door. I looked down and saw my pet cat staring
up at me with her large, sparkling eyes. She
meowed and quietly loped into my dark room. I
slowly shut the door, hoping not to wake anyone. I
turned around and trudged back to my bed, tiredly

laying down and rolling the soft sheets over me and closing my eyes. *Back to thinking,* I thought. My mind began to wander again as a perfect silence filled the room. The silence was interrupted by a meow. I ignored it, but shortly after, I felt tiny paws patting my forehead. I opened my eyes and saw an angry look on my cat's face as she meowed and pawed me.

I began to get very annoyed with her and pushed her gently away, trying to hint to her that I was going to sleep, but she kept meowing and pawing. I tugged the sheets over my head, trying to block out my cat. *What is her problem?* I thought as the meowing continued. I wish I could understand what she wanted. I covered my head in the blankets and drifted to sleep with the sound of meows and the feeling of paws on me.

I awoke to the sound of voices chatting and loud stomping footsteps. I slowly opened my eyes and took a big stretch, still half asleep. I blinked a couple times and yawned as I refocused on my surroundings. I looked up and saw women and men walking around busy streets. I saw huge, tall buildings that stretched far into the sky. There were busy taxis and cars honking angrily. I could feel a howling wind blowing against me, giving me the chills. *Where am I?* I thought. *Am I still dreaming?*

I suddenly started to feel queasy. I felt very hot and sticky, and heavy. Every time I heard a car honk, my ears would ring. I felt speechless. I couldn't wrap my head around how real this dream felt. I decided to try walking. I took one step, slightly wobbling, forward. I looked down at my feet. When I looked down, I saw small, furry, orange paws. I closed my eyes and started to feel nauseous again. I looked down once again, hoping to see my own two feet, but again, only saw paws. I started to walk again, but it felt so different from walking. It was more like crawling. I felt like I was on all fours. I started to worry because what if I wasn't dreaming? But then again, how could this not be a dream? I began to walk forward once more, feeling better now. I tried to figure out why this happened.

I continued to walk around, wondering about what I was. I saw people moving about, and talking on phones. I had to walk carefully through their legs, so I wouldn't get kicked. I smelled hot dogs, and heard cars honking furiously. I started to familiarize myself with my body and vision as I walked faster and more comfortably. The sidewalk I was walking along looked like a never ending stretch of pavement with stomping feet, puddles, and scurrying rats all around me. I felt odd and wet. I looked up and saw many different faces glaring down at me, and heard voices that muttered "pesky cat!" and "move it." I felt a sharp pain hit me in the side as I was launched through the streets. *I have been kicked*, I thought. *Probably by someone who was in a rush.* I landed on my side, in an empty alley. I felt relieved that I wasn't hurt

too badly, but still in pain, as I got up and started walking again. I thought about what I was. I remembered someone glaring down at me and muttering "pesky cat." *Well, that clears everything up...* I thought. *I am a cat. I am Piper.*
The city smelled like smoke and garbage, and the air was thick, making me choke. While I was cautiously walking along, I could see figures wearing dark clothes and smoking, leaned up against walls.
The sky was grey, and the ground was speckled with raindrops. I continued walking, but even faster now. I didn't like this place at <u>all</u>. I turned corners and blocks randomly, trying to find a way out of the smoky, lonely city. I had an odd urge to be in a tight warm place, like a warm laundry basket full of towels. I wished I could be somewhere warm and safe, where I could breathe clean air and where my nose wouldn't be all clogged with smoke. I was tired of smoky air and stomping feet. I felt invisible, so small and helpless in the big city. It seemed like every corner I turned led to more of the same dull city. I walked for what seemed like forever until I heard a voice saying "Hey, hey you, stop!" The voice was coming from <u>my</u> level, and was directed towards me. I paused, and then quickly turned around.
I saw a scrawny grey cat sitting in front of me. He stared deeply into my eyes. Suddenly I heard another voice. "Are you lost?" The raspy voice questioned me.

"Who said that?" I asked, looking around.

"Uh… me" the raspy voice replied. I turned back to the grey cat and stared into his electric blue eyes. *Are you talking to me?* I thought.

"Uh, yes! Who else would be talking to you?" The raspy voice said again.

I stared at the cat while I heard the voice. I couldn't see his mouth moving, but I could sense that he was talking to me. I wondered how we could communicate without talking.

"Follow me" he said to me. He started to tiptoe away slyly. *Should I follow him?* I wondered.

I decided to risk it and follow him. I concentrated on his fast pace so I could keep up with him. We soon arrived at a sewer that was cracked open in an alley. The grey cat crawled into the sewer, and I cautiously followed. My paws felt damp and the air got harder to breathe as we crawled further and further underground.

"Uh, I didn't really catch your name" I said as we continued crawling through the sewer.

"Oh, my apologies, I'm Felix. And you are?"

"Oh, uh, I'm M-Piper" I stuttered.

"Nice to meet you, M-Piper!" Felix laughed. His voice echoed through the sewer.

"Where are we going?" I asked.

"I'll show you. We are almost there!" Felix exclaimed.

We were approaching a turn in the sewer pipe. I began to hear a soft murmuring of voices that got louder and louder as we approached the turn. As we crawled around the turn, I saw cats, at least two hundred of them, lying lazily about on a stone ledge above the stream of sewer water. They all looked very skinny and weak. Some of them were sick.

"Welcome to the clan," Felix grinned.

I took a look around. I looked at the stained floor, which was tinted green. I smelled the horrible overwhelming stench of sewage.

"What is this place?" I wondered.

"Here, I'll show you around," Felix offered. "This is the clan, where all the strays of the city live. We give them a home, so they can rest."

"Stray cats?"

"Yeah, just cats with no homes," Felix explained.

"How many live here?" I asked him.

"Last time we counted… about six hundred seventy. But most of them aren't back yet."

"Oh my goodness!!" I was shocked.

"Yup, it's pretty crazy. The numbers change a lot though. You know strays, we come and go as we choose."

"So…can I live here too now?" I asked hesitantly.

"Yep, welcome!"

Felix showed Piper around the sewers some more.

"Here," he said. "This is where you'll be sleeping!"

Piper lay down on the cold, hard floor, exhausted. After not too long, she fell asleep.

The next day, she woke up and tried to clear her mind from earlier.

"Good Morning Piper!" Felix said.

"What? Where am I?" I stuttered. Felix gave me a puzzled look and continued to say

"Are you okay?" I walked away. I stared at all the skinny starving cats, wishing I could help them. I wanted to help them. I needed to help them.

I left the sewers and joined the bustle of the streets again. Then I looked around for help. "Help," I called. "There are poor starving cats!" I hollered. "Help!" Nobody paid any attention to my rant. *They all just walked past me, as if I didn't even exist!*

I didn't give up. I continued to examine the streets for help. When I saw a strange figure staring at me from across the road, something clicked in my memory. He wore a long jacket with a pin on it. The symbol on that pin… It looked familiar. Then it hit me. It was the same symbol on my wrist! A bus interrupted my thoughts as it zoomed in front of me. I looked across the street again. The man was gone.

I ran across the street and heard cars honking. The sky was grey, and suddenly it began to pour. I started into a full-on sprint. I was confused. *Why did he have the same symbol that I had on my wrist?* I scanned the streets.

Suddenly, I saw him! I kept my eyes on him as I bumped past people on the streets. He quickly turned a corner into an alley, and I kept following him, being careful to keep my distance. He turned into a school next. It was a large public school in

New York City. I followed him into the door. *Where is he going?* I thought to myself. *I have to find help for the cats in the sewer.* Suddenly, a strange sensation came over Piper. Her vision went blurry, and she grew-really fast. She was….stretching….changing. She shifted her paws, trying to balance herself, only…. They weren't paws. *What? Am I..... HUMAN?* "I'm Human!!" she almost blurted before remembering the strange man would hear her. *I'm human now? What is happening? Was it all a dream? Am I Piper again?*

I quickly ducked into the school and used my stealthy cat-like instincts to continue following the man. After following the mysterious man for a long time, we arrived in a strange room that looked as if it had charcoal smudged across the walls. The man stood in the room for a while as I spied on him. His coat was black as pitch, and I got a glimpse of his eyes, which were electric blue. My eyes were still locked on his pin. I looked at my wrist, then at the pin, then at my wrist, then at the pin.

"Hello," a deep voice said from across the room. I quickly looked up, slinking farther behind a desk, making sure not to be seen.

"Hello," the man with the pin said. "I've found all of the victims and labeled them."

The two men spoke for a long while, yet I was still aching for information. They spoke of gathering

146

people with different "powers." This is what they said:

"I've made the clones for the last victim," said the man with the pin.

"Good. How are her morphing skills?" replied the man with the deep voice.

"Weak."

"Mmm. Is she suspicious of the clones?" the man with the pin asked.

"Not a bit, she's very gullible!" the deep voice rumbled.

"Nice job. Now I'd better be off."

I sprinted out of the building, eager to think. Why did I seem to have a constant train of strange thoughts swirling through my head? My mind whirled with questions. Why do they want people with "powers"? Do they want ME? What's with the clones?

BUMP!

I had run into a girl walking down the street. I shook my head and said, "Oh, sorry!" I began to walk past her, but then I noticed something on her wrist.

"Wait!" I yelled to her.

"Um...?" the girl murmured.

I took a moment to examine her. She had shoulder length brown hair, and deep, dark eyes that looked me up and down.

"What do you want?" she asked me.

"Sorry," I began. "I just couldn't help but notice the marking on your wrist."

"Oh, this?" she said. "I was born with it!"
I looked carefully at the marking on her wrist. I held my wrist close to hers. It matched. She had the same marking as me! I began to tell her everything I had heard the men say. I told her because I had a feeling the markings must have something to do with having "powers," or in my case, having the ability to turn into a cat.
"What?!" She said. "I gotta go…"
I ran across the street and in the direction of the sewer. I had to tell Felix about this. As I was running, I felt myself getting smaller… I looked in a store window and saw myself… as a cat. I kept running. I soon made it to the sewer pipe. But, I saw a strange figure climbing into it. It wasn't Felix, it was a human! I scurried down the pipe, chasing the figure. As soon as I made it back to the ledge in the sewer, I found Felix. He was sitting right in front of me. All the other cats were ten feet back from him, also facing me. Dead frozen.
"Oh, I didn't expect you to be here, Piper." Felix stuttered.

Underwater

Izzy Boyle

"How much longer until we leave?" I asked impatiently.

"Fifteen more minutes." my dad answered, annoyed.

It was twelve thirty. A few days ago, my uncle had invited us to spend the week on my uncle's boat. I had been waiting for years to do this, so I was excited.

"Yay, we are here!" I screamed.

"Settle down," my dad demanded.

"Sorry," I said.

When I got out of the car, I ran to my uncle's little boat and gave my uncle a hug.

"Are you ready to go?" my uncle questioned.

"Yes, let's go." I answered back.

When my dad jumped onto the boat, my uncle started the engine, and we were off.

"Do you want to fish?" my uncle asked.

"Sure," I responded.

While my uncle grabbed the fishing line, I saw a whale.

"Here you go," my uncle said as he handed me the fishing line.

I grabbed the fishing line and stepped onto the big stool. I flung the fishing line into the crisp, clean water.

"Be careful," my uncle warned.

"I will be fine," I told my uncle.

I waited for an hour before I felt a tug. At first, it was small, but then it became harder and harder. I relaxed a bit as the line became still again. The next part was a haze of screaming, running and falling. I did not know how to describe it. All I knew was that I was back to life when I hit the rough, dark water.

"Help me!" I yelled as the current pulled me under the water. Down, down, down I went, struggling to make my way up to the surface. Seeing that I was making no progress, I stopped struggling. A minute later, I took a forced breath, expecting to choke. Instead of choking, I actually felt relieved. I took another breath. I could not believe it. I was breathing underwater! When I finally caught my breath, I started to swim again, but the current was too strong. I had to find a way up to the surface. Finally, I caught a current that would take me to the surface. Ten feet from the surface, I took one last breath, but this time I took in a lot of water. Choking, I forced my head through the surface of the water.

"Dad!" I yelled when I caught my breath.

"Over there," I heard my dad tell my uncle.

With all his might, my dad pulled me into the boat.

"How are you still alive?" my dad asked.

"I could breathe underwater." I replied.

"I think she has lost a lot of oxygen," my uncle remarked.

"We need to get her to shore," my dad suggested.

"Well, she is okay." the nurse confirmed. "She just has a couple of bruises and scrapes."

"How could she have survived?" my dad asked.

"Things like this have happened before to other patients. We are not sure if it is true, but I do know that many studies have been done on this." she replied.

"It is time to go," my dad said to me.

I got out of the chair and walked out of the hospital.

"I could breathe underwater." I told my dad.

"Are you sure you did not hit your head?" my dad questioned.

"This is serious, Dad," I said, annoyed.

"Okay," he replied with a hint of confusion.

The whole ride home I explained the amazing story of my underwater experience.

"I still think you are full of baloney," my dad confirmed.

"Believe what you want, but think about it. How else could I have survived underwater for five hours?" I asked.

The look on his face was hard to explain. It was not surprised or angry. It was the look of defeat.

"Good morning," I said as I walked into the kitchen on Saturday morning.

"We are going scuba diving in five minutes," my mom said as she ignored my greeting.

"We need to go," I demanded.

We all got into the car and arrived at the beach
within an hour. I headed to the beach and waited
for a while. After about an hour, I went to see what
was taking so long.

"We have a little problem. One of the scuba masks
is broken, so we can only take one person diving.
So I guess we can..."

"You guys go. I will be fine just waiting here. I am
old enough now," I interrupted.

"I guess dad and I will go scuba diving," my mom
stated.

They got into the water and swam far away from
me. After my dad and mom left, I waited thirty
minutes before I went into the water. I wanted to
make sure that my parents would not see me.
Wearing my school clothes, I hopped into the
water and started to swim into the ocean.

Once I was about twenty feet from the shore, I
dove underwater and saw that sitting at the bottom
of the ocean was a rock that seemed to be made of
gold. Curious, I dove down even further and picked
up the shining rock.

In no time at all, a memory flashed back to me. I
remembered scuba diving with my parents and
finding a rock just like the one that I had just found.
Staring at the rock, I realized that this rock was
only fool's gold, and it wasn't real gold. This was
the same rock that I had found two years ago, and
this was the one that had taught me a valuable
lesson. I had found the rock and had been
convinced that it was really gold. When my dad

took a look at it, he realized that it was not real gold. It was just fool's gold. I was so angry that I grabbed the fool's gold out of his hand and threw it into the water as far as I could.

Seeing that I was angry, my dad had come up to me and said these exact words: "Sometimes you have to let go of the thing that means a lot to you because sometimes things in life don't go your way. Don't let that hold you back."

Knowing my dad was a very poetic person, I didn't believe him. For the next month and a half I was in an angry mood. I got mad at everything anyone did. One day. My dad finally marched into my room and said, "Don't let challenges get into the way of who you are. Sometimes in life you are not going to get your way, and that's okay. You have to enjoy what you have, and not what you don't have.

A sudden rumble awoke me from my daydream. Rocks tumbled around me, and at that moment, I realized that we were having an earthquake. Before I could do anything, rocks came tumbling down from the cliff and took me down farther into the deep blue water. It was too late when I realized that I was being taken down to the bottom. Frantically, I swam under a small opening right below a huge coral wall. About a fourth of a second later, all of the rocks came crashing down less than one inch away from me. I started choking on the bits of debris and rigid rocks that floated in the water. The once clean, pretty water felt dirty and polluted. Once I could breathe again, I searched for an opening. After twenty minutes, I gave up, sitting down in the small space on the bottom of the ocean. I thought of my earliest memories and the most recent ones. I thought about my trip to my uncle's lake and that one time when I got an A on a math test when I had never before gotten an A. It was only then that I realized that the small things in life meant the most to me.

After about four hours, I felt rumbling as the rocks around me began to fall. Covering my head, I desperately tried to push the rocks away from me. Finally, I was able to get out of the hole. Swimming hard, I tried to go away from the area. After one last rumble, the rigid black rocks tumbled down through the water. I watched as the last beautiful rocks fell down, swimming away from them. Certain that no more rocks were falling, I looked closer at the wreckage. The water started to grow darker and darker, and I looked up as the last rock came down right above me. I swam as hard as I could, but the rock hit my head as it started to go the other direction, following the current. I finally reached the shore. I looked at the soft sand. Never in my life had I ever been so glad to see land. After about twenty minutes, I saw my parents walk up. I quickly wiped the drops of blood dripping down the side of my head. My head hurt a lot, but I couldn't let anybody know. All I had ever had to do to get along with everyone was to be tough. I had never complained of a

headache or sore throat. All I had ever known was
to be tough.

"I forgot to tell you, they are tearing down that
coral reef so don't go near there," my dad said in a
guilty tone.

I stared at him, my head full of anger.

"Maybe th-" I stopped myself from yelling. "You
know, Dad, that's okay, we all make mistakes," I
corrected myself.

He smiled.

Acrophobia

Emma Beck

Poppy shivered. She didn't mind the cool breeze swirling overhead. She peeked down over the edge. Unlike the breeze, the edge terrified Poppy. Even more than the edge though, Poppy was afraid of the asphalt ten stories below. You see, Poppy wasn't so much scared of heights, but she was scared of the surface below that she would hit if she fell, and all the open air in-between. Her nightmares were dominated by the edge, the air, the ground. In her dreams, though, the ground was not asphalt, but burning coals, and the fall was often miles long. Just this morning, after another nightmare, Poppy had decided that it was time. It was time to be at peace, time to befriend the edge, and most of all, time to sleep a full night without waking up in a cold sweat, screaming her lungs out. So there she sat, five feet from the edge, shivering as the warm afternoon sunlight beat down on the back of her neck, the breeze ruffling her t-shirt. She sucked in a huge breath and scooted forward a foot. By now, the sun was shining over the trees of the park. Poppy swiped her sweaty palms across her pants. She rubbed her wrist, where a hexagon shaped birthmark crossed her skin. It was a nervous habit. She crossed her arms in front of her to keep herself from rubbing it. The last rays of sunlight peaked out from over the tops of the trees, and Poppy squeezed her eyes shut tightly. It was now or never. She placed her hands on the cold concrete behind her. By now, they had gone a splotchy, red, white and purple color, half from fear and half from the early evening cold. She slid forward and yelped as her feet collided with thin air. She opened her eyes slowly and tried to calm her breathing. In, out… in, out… in, out… much better. Her ankles lay just over the edge. If she could only get her legs to scoot a little bit further over the edge.

Suddenly she slipped off the edge. Her breath caught in her throat. *Oh-no!* she thought. *I never meant to fall. Is this it? Am I going to die? Will I never see my mom or my dad or my best friend, Wilma, again? What am I going to do?* She realized her eyes were squeezed closed. *Wait a second. That's weird…there's no wind. Shouldn't I have hit the ground by now?* Poppy opened her eyes. She gasped. She was sitting outside her apartment deck- in the air. She squeaked in surprise. *Oh, that's interesting,* she thought. She waved her arm under her foot and…there was nothing there. She was flying. She started to sway, and then, *whoops!* She flipped upside down. The blood rushed to her head and she could see the ground a few stories below spinning under her. *I'm up really high…but I'm not afraid!* she thought. The all-too-familiar swooping in her stomach was there, yes, but it wasn't a scared sort of feeling; it was an excited one. She imagined herself swooping gracefully over to the railing of her balcony, and the air moved under her, propelling her. She climbed over the railing. Her feet hit the deck, and a wash of heaviness returned to her limbs. *I hope I can do that again. It's so much more comfortable than this in the air, weightless...oh, well.*

Poppy walked back into her apartment. Creak . . . Bang! The screen door snapped behind Poppy, and she hurried to close the rusty metal door on top of it. In a puff, the cold air from outside was obliterated.

The warm, savory smell of dinner came in from the kitchen. Poppy flopped down onto a beige armchair. Most of her apartment was beige. The walls were beige, the chairs were beige, and even the kitchen counter was a sickly shade of beige. Poppy heard her dad clunking pots into the sink and turning on the spray function of the faucet. Every time he walked past the doorway, his shadow danced into the living room, then up the wall. Then it was gone. The sun, having just gone down, caused the living room to be very dark. Her dad had been too busy in the kitchen making dinner to turn on the light. Poppy was deciding whether or not she should go and turn the light on when she closed her eyes and fell asleep.

"Poppy, it's dinnertime," Dad said.

Poppy opened one eye. "What?" she croaked.

"It is time for dinner. Come wash up before we eat. Mom is home."

"What time is it?"

"Seven thirty," Dad smiled. "I thought you could use the sleep. Come and eat now."

Poppy groaned and rolled off the chair. She flipped onto the floor with a soft thud. She pulled out one of the beige dinner chairs next to her mom, who was reclining with her eyes closed and chatting with her dad. Poppy remained groggy, and there was a funny taste in her mouth. She shoveled homemade macaroni and cheese into her mouth methodically.

"Mmph," she mumbled.

"Yes, Poppy?" her mom smiled.

Poppy swallowed hurriedly, clearing her mouth. "Thanks for the macaroni n' cheese, Dad."

"I'm glad you like it."

Poppy spooned the last warm, cheesy morsel into her mouth. She pushed her chair back from the table, brushed her teeth, and stumbled back into the living room. The couch pulled out into a third bed for the one-bedroom apartment, and Poppy climbed under her quilt.

The next morning was cool and breezy. The sun smiled down on all the little people of the city. Spring was definitely in the air. Even Poppy's beige apartment had an air of freshness to it. Poppy rolled out of bed and padded into the kitchen to grab a bowl of cereal. Her dad had left early in the morning for work, like usual. He was a clerk at the local Wal-Mart. Her mom had had a long day yesterday, so she would not wake up until at least eight o'clock.

Poppy dressed and hopped into the living room, pulling on her left sock. She was not looking at where she was going, and she tripped over her boots, which were strewn on the rug. Picking one up, she noticed brown mud caked on the sole. She absentmindedly flicked it off and pulled on her other sock. It took her thirty seconds to pull on her boots and lace them up, and then she scribbled a note to her mom:

Mom, I'm at the park with Wilma. I will be back by 9.

Flap, flap, flap! Wilma and Poppy ran along the sidewalk dodging pedestrians.

"What's that noise?" Poppy asked.

"What noise?" Wilma replied.

"It sounds like flap, flap, flap."

"Oh, that's my sneaker. Frederick got it. (Frederick was Wilma's Chihuahua.)

"How did he fit that thing into his mouth? It's like twice his size!"

"I don't know, his jaw must have unhinged or something. So what is this important-enough-to-wake-me-before-noon thing you were going to tell me?"

Poppy glanced around them. The sidewalk was full of people, but no one seemed to be paying them any attention.

"Well, you're not going to believe this, but yesterday I fell off the balcony."

"I don't follow you."

"The balcony. You know, the one outside my apartment?"

"Yeah."

"I fell off of it."

"You fell off your deck, which is like ten stories high. You are kidding me!"

"Nope, I am totally serious."

"Yeah right, there is no way that's even possible."

"That's exactly why I told you!"

"Uh-huh. So, if you really did fall from the balcony and you survived without a scratch, you won't mind if I push you down the storm drain. Just for kicks, you know. And maybe you'll think twice about waking me up to tease me?"

"Wilma, I'm serious. I get that it's difficult to believe and all, but I swear I'm telling the truth."

Wilma looked skeptical.

"Here, I have an idea. Come with me." Poppy said, quickening her pace and turning onto Eleventh Street.

A few minutes later, Wilma and Poppy arrived at a large wrought iron gate.

"Why are we at the park?" Wilma asked as a jogger ran past wearing a purple athletic shirt and Nikes, listening to her iPod as she ran. Across a green field of grass with carefully positioned oak trees was a large playground. Red slides and blue swings reflected the glare from the sun. All around the field stretched a paved sidewalk. A kid tossed a

Frisbee to his friend on the grass. Poppy glanced at Wilma.

"I already told you. I have an idea." She set off across the field, heading straight toward the playground. Wilma ran to catch up with Poppy. She got to the start of the wood chips when Poppy began climbing up the steps of the playground set.

"Poppy, wait for me!" Wilma called.

Poppy climbed onward.

"No really! Wait for me!"

Poppy didn't answer. She had reached the top of the stairs by now.

"Poppy, come back here!"

Poppy turned left and approached the fire pole.

"Wait . . . NO POPPY DON'T DO IT! I BELIEVE YOU! JUST DON'T DO IT! NO! NO, POPPY STOP!" Wilma yelled. The boy with the Frisbee looked over at them with a weird expression on his face.

Poppy had reached the fire pole and was sliding her feet off the edge so that they dangled in the air. Wilma ran over to her.

"Wow, Poppy! Don't do that! You scared me! I thought you were going to, like, take a flying leap off the play set. I worried about your sanity for a second there." She paused. "What *are* you doing, anyway?"

Poppy was now hanging by her fingertips from the play set. She smiled.

"Watch this."

She let go. Her arms immediately felt more comfortable. They had been hurting from hanging like that, and the blood had drained out of them. She started to feel dizzy. The wind picked up speed. She had been in the air for four or five seconds! That was way too long. She was spinning now, faster and faster, her hair whipping around her face. Then, just as the wind began to die down, Poppy opened her eyes. She was flying. Wilma shrieked. "OMG, Poppy! That is so cool!"

She clapped her hands. Poppy floated a little bit higher. Wilma ran over and grabbed onto her ankles. Poppy hoped she would be able to carry Wilma, but she brushed away the thought. She would stay low. They rose up high enough that Wilma was right above the ground and moved forward across the playground. Poppy looked around the playground. She felt so tall . . . and well, weightless. Everyone else was so short. *Everybody else!* She shook Wilma off her feet and dropped with a thud.

"Ow!" Wilma said indignantly. "Why did you do that?"

"Wilma, we are in public."

"Oh yeah. We don't want to let anybody in on your amazingness. How long have you known?"

"Twelve hours."

"Why didn't you call me earlier?"

"I was not sure whether or not I could do it again."

"Can I do it?"

"I don't know. Go ahead and try."

Wilma jumped into the air and came down hard. "Nope, it doesn't work for me," she said.

"I'm sorry. I can take you anywhere you want, though. I don't mind. You don't weigh anything in the air."

"Thanks Pop. So, what are we going to do about this?" Wilma asked as they walked out of the park toward home.

"What do you mean? We can't really *do* anything."

"Pop, you don't understand! You're, like, supernatural. This is way too big of a secret to keep. We have to tell *somebody*."

"No, Wilma, I don't want you to tell anyone. Sure, tell your family, but no one else! I mean, seriously. Think about it. Think about everything we could do with this."

"Like what?"

"Well, for one thing, I could be an Olympic athlete. I could ice skate, or do gymnastics. My jumps and flips would be gold medal winners. I could get rich doing shows. I could be a millionaire! Of course, you could be my most trusted assistant. It'd be so fun!" Poppy smiled crookedly. "We could do anything, Wilma!"

Wilma's smile was plastered to her face. Most trusted assistant? Poppy's great plans didn't seem to have much need for an assistant. Her being rich and famous was really sort of a one-man show. Why would Wilma want to be second-best all her life, anyway? *Why is Poppy so special?* Wilma thought. *Why didn't I get superpowers, too?*

164

Poppy frowned. "Wilma, are you alright?" Poppy asked, pulled out of her fantasies. Wilma appeared lost in thought, and she had a distinct frown.

"What? Oh yeah. Poppy, I was just thinking."

"So, what do you think? What should we use the power for?"

A spark of jealousy flared up in the back of Wilma's mind. "Uh, I think I need to go home now. Let's talk later," she said.

"Okay, bye Wilma."

The girls parted, Wilma walking down one street and Poppy down another. Poppy kicked a stone with her toe. It skidded off the sidewalk and came to rest in a puddle of grime and gasoline. Why had Wilma left? Poppy knew her too well to be deceived by her quick fib. If she hadn't needed to return home, why had she left? Was it something Poppy had said? Maybe she had just felt sick, but . . . no; she would have just said so. Was Wilma afraid of Poppy's power? Poppy really hoped not. After all, she didn't know if it was reversible. She had been so excited to show Wilma her power that she hadn't even considered that Wilma might be afraid of it.

Poppy, lost in thought, hadn't realized where she was going. She was now in an alley between two apartment buildings. Garbage lay in heaps on the soiled street. Tiny rivulets of runoff trickled across the pavement. Poppy was just turning around to retrace her steps, when in a blur of motion; something whizzed from a nearby trash heap and caught her on the shoulder. She peered down at a tiny dart lodged in her shoulder. Her vision blurred and random colors swam before her eyes. She crumpled to her knees and everything went dark.

Poppy groaned. Her head ached. Her arms were twisted into an uncomfortable position. Something was cutting into her ankles. She opened one eye and winced at the sight of her legs bound tightly to a wooden bedpost. She was sprawled on a rough concrete floor, and a large bruise on her forearm gave her the notion that she hadn't been placed there gently. She tried to remember . . . what had happened? Where was she? Her brain was really foggy and befuddled. It hurt more when she strained to think. Suddenly it came to her. She remembered walking down the alley. A net had fallen down onto her from the window above her. Then, something had landed on her. She looked down at her shoulder, where a small pinprick was visible, surrounded by a red welt. Ah . . . she had been drugged, probably by an anesthetic dart. That was why her head was so achy, and it was so hard to think straight.
But then, why was she wrapped up in a net? She would have been such an easy target for a dart, just walking along aimlessly. When the net fell on her, however, she had thrashed about uncontrollably. Wouldn't a kidnapper (Poppy assumed that she had been kidnapped) want to have good aim when

he/she shot the dart? The net seemed so pointless.
As if Poppy was going to run away with an
anesthetic kicking in, let alone tangled in fishing
net! What did this kidnapper even want from her?
Most kidnappings that she'd heard about were
unplanned. An adult would see a kid alone on a
street and lure her into his car with, say candy. The
stereotypical white-van creeper.
Poppy hadn't been lured, though. She had just
happened to walk into the alley. It was so unlikely.
This mysterious person must have been following
her. But why didn't he/she go creeper-style and
just stick her in a car? Why drop a net over her? It
must have been very difficult to set up the net and
get ready to dart her on a minute's notice. Speaking
of the dart, Poppy realized that it had come from a
trash pile; a moment after the net was dropped
from a one-story window. There must have been at
least two people involved, one to drop the net, and
one to dart her. This kidnapping was becoming
more and more peculiar. Why follow her around?
Why not just push her into a van? Why were two
or more people involved? Why choose Poppy?
Why the net?
Suddenly, a realization struck Poppy. These people,
they *knew*. They knew about her "gift". It made
total sense. The net was meant to stop her from
flying away when they tried to kidnap her. They
needed two people, maybe more because they
thought she was dangerous. Poppy smiled to
herself as she imagined a whole army of

167

kidnappers struggling to catch her as she rose into the sky. They needed her because she was different. She was special. They had to follow her around because they couldn't settle for just anyone. It had to be her. Suddenly fearful, she glanced around her cell. What were they going to do to her? She had to escape. She checked for her phone, but of course, it was no longer in her pocket. They must have taken it away from her.

She huffed. Just her luck. Her brow furrowed, and she stood up, reaching out for the padded walls. Wait. Padded walls? Poppy dug her fingers into the thick layer of blue foam. It was extremely soft. Why pad the walls of a prison cell? Maybe to keep prisoners who had been captive for so long they'd gone insane from hurting themselves. But . . . if that was true, they would have at least made the padding stronger. This stuff was so soft she could break if off with her hands. A memory flickered at the back of her mind. What was it? Something about foam . . . oh! Yes, the trip she had taken in fourth grade to see a famous recording studio. The name escaped her. The walls of the audio booth had been coated in a similar, foam-like substance, and the tour guide had talked at length about how the foam absorbed any sound up to one hundred and fifty decibels. The man had let the children, in turn, go into the room and scream as loud as they could. Nobody outside could hear it. Poppy remembered how scared she had been imagining getting locked into the room, where nobody could

hear her screaming. *Sounds familiar,* she thought.
That was why she was in a foam-encased,
soundproof room- so she would be helpless.
Actually, this small bit of information was rather
helpful. If her captors had needed to make her cell
soundproof that meant there must be someone
outside to hear her. If she was all alone, they
wouldn't have bothered with the soundproofing.
She picked away at the foam layer, digging deeper
and deeper, until she reached rough plaster. A large,
fluffy blue pile had accumulated by her feet, and
her clothes were covered in blue dust.
She took a bobby pin out of her hair and started to
chip away at it. Bit by bit, small clouds of white
powder puffed away from the wall.

Wilma's thoughts swirled onto the paper. She was
oblivious of the blue park bench and the city
dwellers around her. Her pencil slid across the
page, shading and scratching. Her mind was at
peace, her world momentarily revolved only
around this one drawing, and she smiled. It showed
a leopard and a raven in a field of tall grass. At the
bottom was written: I'm so glad you're my friend.
She folded it into an envelope. Addressing it, she
got up and took off at a run.

"Poppy, good morning." Poppy's mom yawned.
She thumped down the stairs and rubbed her eyes.

She blinked. Why was there a pile of blankets on the floor? Where was Poppy?

"Poppy?" she called. She poked her head into the bathroom. It was empty. She walked back into the kitchen, and her hand brushed a scrap of paper. On the paper, a note was written in Poppy's signature scrawl. This is what it said:

Mom, I'm at the park with Wilma. I will be back by 9.

Poppy's mom looked at the clock on the beige wall. It was ten thirty. Poppy's mom sat down at the kitchen table, a crease forming on her forehead.

"Wilma, thank goodness! Poppy's mom just called. We were just about to go looking for you girls. What were you thinking?" her mom asked. Wilma had just stepped into her doorway and was currently being bombarded with relieved voices.

"Sorry I'm late. I had to send a letter."

Her dad frowned. "Wilma, it is eleven thirty! You said you'd be back soon. You've been gone four hours. We were going to call the police. We tried to call you, but your phone was dead. I'll go call Poppy's parents now and let them know that she's on her way," he said, pulling out his cell phone. "Hello? Hi, Nancy. Wilma just got home, and she says Poppy's on her way. Yes. No. Uh-huh. Of course, we're really grateful. Yup. Okay, bye." He turned to Wilma and her mom.

"Poppy's not home, yet. What time would you say she left the park, Wilma?"

"She left at about nine o'clock."

Poppy's arm ached. Her fingers were raw. She had reached a smooth steel wall. It was hopeless. A tear rolled down her cheek. She slumped against the wall and slid to the floor. With a soft creak, the barred door opened, and a man stepped through it.

"You needn't cry, dear," he smiled.

His hair was black and slicked back with plenty of hair gel. He had one green eye and one blue eye, and a tiny little spot of a beard right on his chin. He looked familiar. Dr. Telmer. That was his name. Poppy was sure. How did she know this? She was starting to get a headache. Dr. Telmer walked into her cell. He raised his eyebrows at the sight of her handiwork on the wall.

"Well, well. That's very nice, dear. But, alas, we already thought of that."

Poppy wiped angrily at her wet face. She needed to please this man. She needed to obey him. No matter what, she must obey.

"That's better," the man smiled. "Welcome home, dear. We have a lot of work to do."

The Reckoning

Bryce Danosky

As I trudged silently along the dirty wet and cluttered sidewalks of Seattle with my friend David, who was always brooding and kept to himself, yet was valedictorian every year. I had never belonged with any of the cliques at school. I wasn't a nerd, a geek, a gamer, or a popular kid. I was normal, never fitting in, while David, *David*, he fit in with everyone. He carried himself with a natural grace and confidence that portrayed something extra, an aura of strength that he exuded, strengthening those around him. Giving him the impression of invincibility, with his black, cropped hair and tanned skin. Next to him, and almost anyone I was nondescript, invisible with my light brown hair, dark eyes, unassuming features, and to top it all off I was short. We continued down the well worn dry, cracked sidewalk. Our feet scuffling, our backs hunched from the weight of our packs. When we reached the intersection that separated the slums from the suburbs, I turned left as David turned right. Before we got far I said, "Later David," and he responded with, "See you tomorrow, Adam." As I meandered down the sidewalk deeper and deeper into the slums I was accosted by a gang member, about 18, with bulging muscles and a lean form. He wore a black hoodie and jeans with a balaclava adorning his head. I stood there for a moment vacillating, deciding whether to run or leave myself open to a beating. As he slowly approached, seemingly with a deadly intent, I began to turn and run. When I completely turned I heard him call out, "Wait kid, I have a proposition." I continued turning to look back at him and raise my eyebrow, and state flatly, "Continue," He grinned and said, "We know what your Dad has been doing to you, I am giving you this offer to join our ranks." I began to turn again; he tried one last time, "On a trial basis, with pay." Wordlessly I continued to stride away without looking back. I heard him sigh and walk away, as he did he shouted, "Two days, corner of Stratford and 116th." I continued walking and walking until houses became shoddy trailers. I saw my home, a small trailer with a porch where my Dad was sitting, in a small woven rocking chair, beer bottle in hand. I hurriedly began turning around, praying he hadn't seen me. That was when I heard, words slurred, "Get back hear kid." Was that my name now, kid? Taking a deep breath and turning around I walked back into view. He beckoned to me with his beer bottle, sloshing a small amount over the rim. I trudged forward and stepped heavily onto the porch. Thankfully, he stayed calm, at least for a moment. I stepped up for a moment and his convincing façade dropped. Despite his slovenly, round appearance and balding head he moved deceptively quickly. His fist, thankfully not his bottle, smashed my jaw throwing me off the porch. He sneered, "Learned your lesson yet kid, I told

you to get back before six. I started hauling myself
to my feet. "Dad don't be unreasonable," I pleaded,
"You know how long of a walk it is." I began
massaging my jaw and stepped up to the door. As I
did he barred my way baring his teeth menacingly.
"I don't think you've learned your lesson yet," he
snarled, "No dinner or bed for you tonight, now off
my property!" he screamed, spittle hitting my face.
I turned head held high and walked across the
gravel. I heard a peculiar whistling sound and I
tilted my head trying to discern what it was. As I
did, a bottle flew by my left ear, impacting the
gravel and shattering. I walked away without
looking back. Slowly I realized that I had had
enough of his antics. My mind continued to drift
back to my conversation with the gang member or,
"ganger," for short. Head held high I stalked away
determined to never return. As I continued walking
I realized that I had nowhere to go. I wandered
aimlessly, bewildered and stung by what my father,
my father had done. Why?! I realized that I had a
loyal friend who I could call on when I needed him.
I began trudging in the direction of the suburbs,
when I came to the realization that I had actually
never been to his home. A friend who had pulled
me through all of those years of torture with my
father, and had always been ready to lend a hand
when I needed him, yet I had no idea where he
lived. I needed to find him, or I would be found by
a ganger. I slowly began increasing my pace as
darkness began to fall over the streets. I finally

crossed the intersection between the suburbs and the slums and gradually the houses became showing finer and finer quality. The evening began to fade into night and the temperature dropped quickly. An odd pressure began to build up in my head as I became more and more desperate. I continued walking and the houses continued growing, until they seemed to be worth millions of dollars. The pressure continued to grow until my head felt as if it was going to burst. I dropped to my knees in pain, the pressure still building, and building. When... I felt something snap and the pressure vanished. When it vanished I heard something from one of the houses to my right.

Before I was pulled up the stairs I had one last question for David, "What can I do and how do I use what I have?"

"You are telekinetic and telepathic."

"What the heck is that?"

"It means you can move things with your mind, and read other peoples thoughts. "

I was jolted from our conversation, my mind reeling as I was dragged up the stairs roughly. At the top there was a lavishly furnished room, with thick shag carpeting, large couches, and curtains that looked as though they were made with gold thread. Just then I noticed a girl about my age standing in the corner, looking afraid. Each one of the men had a name tag, the first reading John Doe, the second man's name was Harry Telmer, and the last was Evan Smith. Telmer started talking first, "Where have you been, you were supposed to be here more than three months ago, that's how we progr-"

"SHUT UP!" yelled Evan, "When are you going to learn to keep your mouth shut.

"But, I was just…" stuttered Telmer.

"Yeah I know rambling… What… a… surprise," Evan stated drily.

Now John Doe interjected his voice surprisingly deep, "Can we please focus and get back to what is supposed to be the point of the conversation?"

With his comment they turned back to me and before they began talking something Telmer said struck me as odd. It almost sounded as if he was going to say programmed.

I began fidgeting as I began to realize that David may have been correct about the men.

My attention shifted to the girl sitting in the back of the room. She had brown hair and striking green eyes. I decided I did not like these men and I was going to get myself, David and the girl out of this place. The men continued talking to each other, but they lowered their volume, and I could not hear them. I had a moment of inspiration, and I focused on the area of my head that I think I remember the pressure originating from. I tried to clear my mind, and all I wanted to do was to talk with the girl. However, while I was lost in my mind, one of the men, Mr. Telmer, walked up and swung his fist into the side of my face. I had never been struck harder, and as I fell to the ground, my attention diverted from the girl directly to Mr. Telmer. The pressure I had been accumulating flowed out, but for the first time, it came out in a wave that I had control of, and I loosed it at Mr. Telmer. The wave directly hit Telmer, and then hit the other two men, and they were actually thrown out of the window, Mr. Telmer flew straight into the window shattering the glass, cutting himself in the process. The other two men flew out as well. Telmer hit the ground with a sickening thud; the man afterward did as well. The final man out the window seemed to regain his wits in mid-air, and he actually stopped… in the air only feet from the ground. He floated back up to look at me. I concentrated on that pressure and I formed the pressure into an arm and grabbed Evan, who was flying, with the arm of energy. I wrapped him up and slammed him into the ground. He went down to the ground with the others. He seemed to make it harder, as if he had resisted my arm of energy. I beckoned to the girl who was staring at me with something resembling awe. She slowly got up. "Hurry up please," I asked in a strained voice. She grinned at me as if sharing in her own private joke, "I'll be there in a sec." Her voice was soft and quiet. I tried one more time, but before I could start talking she was shaking her head. I have to grab something. Before I could turn my head, a blur of light rushed past me. The girl was gone. Now it was my turn to stand with my jaw hanging open with shock. I shook my head and I jogged down the stairs, forgetting about the members of the gang. They had set up around the stairs and as soon as I stepped around, an antsy soldier fired his carbine (Semi-Automatic Rifle) three times in quick succession. Thankfully, his nerves also caught up to his trigger finger, and he shot to my left. However, I was not the only person who had made a mistake. They had apparently forgotten about David. I heard a loud screech from around the corner. Screams began emanating around the building. Every one of these screams was paired with a sickening crunch. I worked up the nerve to look around the corner, but I heard an assault rifle open up and I jerked my head back, but almost immediately the shooting was extinguished. I looked around the corner to see a figure kneeling in the middle of the room. "It" was covered in blood, and there were figures with pools of red around them, lying motionless on the ground.

We walked out of the warehouse and into the street. We put our arms around David and discreetly walked on the edge of the sidewalk, concealing David as much as we could, for he was covered with blood. In his white shirt, we drew curious, scared, and worried glances. Several people began to glance at us. Some drew out phones and through quick glances we all conveyed the same message, we need to find somewhere to lay low. I had a moment of inspiration, I focused on that corner in my head and I sent the tendrils, which I could now sense, directly into their brains. Suddenly I could sense their thoughts as if they were my own. Conversing, we all ended up mutually walking to the school. For what reason?

David's opinion was that we needed to go to the school because he considered it the only safe place to be in our situation.

Sasha wanted to go because she agreed with David, even if she had never been, apparently she trusted his judgment.

I wanted to go for David's reason as well.

After our conferral we realized we had the same opinions. We turned down the road to our school, when a black Hummer, three large black sedans, and a black van rumbled down the road. The sedans purring with the unmistakable sound of power, the Hummer roaring, and the van, well the van just trundled along. Seeing them we all started and jumped away from our huddle. We held our breath when I noticed that the driver of the Hummer was peering out of his window at us. He started and put something to his mouth. Once again

I had to physically remember to connect to his mind. I sent a tendril out and I had a flash of words enter my mind, as if my own. "Go around the corner, U-turn, and apprehend the suspects." All I heard after that was, "Yes sir, right away sir." I turned to David, "We have to run." Unquestioning, he broke into a sprint, just as I did. A moment later, in a flash, Sasha caught up to us. Breathless she asked, "What's going on?"

Short of breath I briefly answered, "Those cars, they are going around the corner and turning back."

Several seconds later she pointed to a driveway,

"Jump that way." One by one we jumped over a small hedge and lay there quietly, just as the front of a sedan edged around the corner with a hum. Silently we lay there as the cars nosed past. Unconsciously, I connected again with the driver of the Hummer, and this time he was being berated as he was reporting that he lost us. The cars all turned around, all but the van. I expected people to hop out and look for us, but dogs also were taken out of the back of the van. In front of each dog's nose a scrap of cloth was held. They shook their heads, put their noses to the sidewalk, and began to make their way here. When they were within fifteen feet they began barking and running at us. We jumped up and ran. The dogs gave chase. David slammed his fist to the sidewalk, and sent out a spray of concrete at the dogs. Whining, confused they stopped for a moment, tripping their masters. I wrapped the pieces in a bubble of my "Telekinetic Energy." I threw it in the dog's direction, cutting them and their masters. We all ran as one of the men drew a pistol. Reflexively, I threw my hand up to block the shot. Instead of blocking the shot, a telekinetic tendril reached out from my hand and grabbed his pistol, ripping it, and two of his fingers right… off… of his… hand. He screamed in pain, and one of the men ran to help him. Sick to my stomach, and reeling, overcome with nausea, I ran away. I caught up to David and Sasha. I looked back and realized that two men and three dogs were still following us. We kept running. The bleeding dogs, with their lolling tongues, rapidly began to outpace us. Sasha turned back, became a blur, and sent a dog flying with… a kick. She was moving so fast I couldn't quite make it out. However, two of the dogs continued to gain on us. Sasha was nearly doubled over, tired. The school was at the end of the next block and we had run five. We reached the school with the dogs on our heels. One of them, the unlucky one, caught up to David and leapt on his back, expecting him to fall over, digging its teeth into David's shoulder. Without breaking stride David reached back, grabbed the dog, and smashed it into the pavement, spraying blood across the sidewalk, breaking many bones, and leaving it a limp mess on the pavement. Still running we reached the school, and turned around to face the last two dogs, and two people. Sasha doubled over in the back breathing heavily. David grabbed the first dog, and threw it at the two men who were still a block away. The dog hit them knocking them down to the pavement. I grabbed the last dog by the leg, and broke it, crippling it. The two men left took one look at the carnage, and ran away as fast as their legs could carry them. Turning to the doorway of the school we walked in and saw an odd green light emanating from a hallway to the right. So, we walked that way. A kid was already walking that way, on a Saturday. She stopped for a second, and then disappeared. Warily, we walked to the doorway emanating the light, opened the closed door, and cautiously entered.

THE AGENCY
Written collaboratively by
Emma, Reina, Ashley, Kira, Izzy, Gaelan, Joey, Sarah,
Grace, Bryce, and Boone

The helicopter tilted and Poppy was pressed against the window. She looked down at the glittering sea hundreds of feet below her and smiled. She was not afraid of heights anymore. The sun was about halfway through the sky. *I wonder how long I was at the Agency,* Poppy pondered. *I was kidnapped at about ten-o-clock, and I'm so tired, it must have been a few days.* The drone of the helicopter blades was like a stick poking into Poppy's back, reminding her that she was far from free. The turquoise water was right below her, if she could just get out of the plane, she could fly home...but of course, that was not a possibility. Poppy chastised herself. *That's wishful thinking. You know there's no way out.* She sighed. She remembered Mr. Telmer entering her cell. She had recognized him, in the way that you would recognize an old family friend or a nanny from your childhood. Mr. Telmer was no nanny. He was her father, in a way. More like her programmer. *I'm not natural,* Poppy thought. Mr. Telmer had explained everything to Poppy. Thirteen years ago, after the Agency had pinpointed all of the "kinetic anomalies..." (They claimed there were more gifted children like Poppy. Strange.) They had used some DNA samples to create an artificial DNA string. That was what Poppy was- an artificial DNA string. The Agency had created her, along with another child who apparently was telekinetic, to lead the others (if there were others) to the Agency building so

183

that they could be finished off before they "got out of hand." Poppy wondered what that meant. Stripping the kids of their powers? Perhaps…no, the Agency wouldn't go so far as to *kill* the kids, would they? Of course they wouldn't. Poppy shook her head to clear her doubts. She could see Mr. Telmer sitting across from her in the helicopter. He seemed like a pretty nice guy. Poppy couldn't help liking him. She wanted to do as he asked. After all, he had created her. He must be very kind and helpful. He was on the good side. He would lead her to victory, if only she would do as he asked. It all came down to her doing as he asked. *But, Poppy! You don't have any choice,* said a small voice in the back of her head. *He's controlling you. Remember, he tweaked your genetic code. You have to do whatever he asks.* You *didn't want to lead these kids to their deaths.* You *didn't agree to find them all in their school and help them get to the agency.* You *never wanted to finish them off. They're just kids, like you. They're innocent.* Poppy bit the inside of her cheek. She was starting to get a headache. Suddenly, the helicopter descended onto the landing strip. The blades slowed down to a soft hum.

"We're here. Get out, number 96," Mr. Telmer said, pulling Poppy back to the present. She felt herself getting up and stiffly jumping out of the helicopter. *If there was a huge flood right now, I would have to just stand here and wait for it to wash me away. I couldn't run unless Mr. Telmer let me. Help.*

"Hurry up, 96. We haven't got all day. Oh, that's right…" Poppy was forced into an awkward trot. She glanced helplessly at the open sky. Freedom was so close. And yet, there was no way she was going to escape. Poppy thought about the poor kids she was going to have to lead to the Agency. If there was a fight, she would be rooting for the kids. Maybe if Telmer died, she could be free. His voice crept into her mind, swirling and twisting her thoughts. No, she did not like these kids. Mr. Telmer was on the good side. The Agency was good. But in the farthest corner of her mind, a tiny thought still pushed through the turmoil. Her subconscious mind was still rooting for the kids, cheering them on. *Please win... Please win... Please win...*

It had been months since Meri had escaped from the asylum. Now she knew how to use her power, and she practiced in her free time until she perfected it. In fact, she had even figured out how to get back in present time so that only seconds had passed since she had left. (She had done this on a quiet Sunday evening by jumping a rift with a stopwatch going.)

Today she was working as a substitute teacher at Pine View Middle School. (She had quit her job at the diner because she had hated it all along.) Right now was her planning period so she had roughly an hour of time to kill since her lesson plan was quite simple. This was due to the fact that the absent teacher had mysteriously disappeared for "personal matters" and had left a couple of work sheets on genetic mutations. It did not look like the teacher had planned to leave because all of his belongings had been left in the classroom, and papers had been strewn across his desk. The teacher, who she presumed was Mr. Telmer because of the name printed on the plaque on his desk, seemed to be quite well known because many teachers had come in asking for him and muttering things like, "not now" or "it couldn't have been," or even "honestly, this is preposterous."

Anyway, Meri had time to kill, so she decided to do some exploring of the school. She had heard from another teacher in the staff room that there was an abandoned classroom where a science experiment had gone horribly wrong. She was pretty sure they had said it was in the 400's wing, so she made her way over.

Immediately, she could feel it. Something about the way the air hung around her like a dusty curtain, the funny feeling in her gut... There was no way to mistake this for a normal classroom. The window in the door was shattered, and there was caution tape draped over the walls. This was obviously the place the teachers had been talking about.

As she approached the door, a strange feeling came over her. She should jump a time rift. Why she felt this way, she did not know, but funny feelings usually had meaning, so she decided to jump.

Now that she knew how to jump time rifts, she was much more aware of her surroundings. The rifts were almost invisible and only detectable by a slight shimmer in the air. When the rift was created, she felt a jumping sensation in her chest. It was what she had mistaken for her heart skipping a beat previously. Going through the rift was almost unnoticeable. One second, she was in this time, the next, she was in another time.

Sometimes, she would aim for a certain time, but this time, she let fate control the outcome. She landed milliseconds later looking at the long rectangular window, once dingy and shattered, but now new and complete. She peered through the window at the busy children rushing around with trays of test tubes and beakers clutched in their hands. The door was cracked open and the hum of excitement surrounded her as she was drawn in...

Two teachers stood with their backs to the door. They appeared to be having a heated conversation in whispers. Occasionally, one would shout out "Careful

188

Davis!" or "Slowly, John" or "Easy does it." She did not blame them, for the class was becoming increasingly hectic. As the whispers intensified, she strained her ears to hear what they were saying.
"Do you think we'll get caught?"
"Relax Rodburg, nobody comes around here at this time," said the second. They both turned to glance at the door, and she ducked just in time. She waited a good thirty seconds before daring to come back up and peek through the window. The teachers had focused their attention back to their conversation.

Meri scanned the students when something caught her eye. It was almost as if it happened in slow motion. Two children who were lab partners were at the end of a very long table towards the back of the classroom. One of them had bright red hair. The red-headed girl was focused intently on the boy who had a goofy grin and seemed to be telling a joke. She threw back her head laughing, and the boy snorted, collapsing onto the table in a fit of giggles, and knocking their tray onto the floor. The boy who told the joke had been smiling triumphantly at the success of his joke. His face quickly fell when he saw the spilled tray and beakers. Apparently, he was not the only one who noticed as a girl shrieked in terror at the spectacle that was yet to become.
Whatever was in the two vials, it was not meant to be mixed.
When the bluish liquid met the orange liquid, it began to smoke and spark. The floor where the liquid had been was gone, and flames were beginning to lick the sides of the

table. Kids screamed and ran around in a state of panic. The fire alarm went off, and one of the teachers swore loudly. The chaos dissipated as the kids lined up by the door. Meri turned the corner and hid as the class emptied out into the hallway. After everyone had left, she walked back through the rift, making sure to concentrate on getting back to the right time. Once she was in present time, she walked back to her classroom, sat down in her seat, and began correcting worksheets. Today was going to be a long day…

Audrey opened the door with the trident inside a hexagon marked on it. She probably would get in trouble if she got caught near this door, nonetheless opening the door, but she was compelled to go inside. It was as if her own mark-matching the symbol on the door-was pulling her towards the room, despite the possibility of getting in trouble.

She peeked inside the room and gaped in awe at the inside area. The room was rather large with charred dark ugly green walls, with a big explosion-looking shape on the wall, and in the middle of the whole room were nine other people. Eight kids and one adult were together, chattering like little birds, and surprise filled her even more as she glanced over every person.

Audrey recognized every child there-Holly, of course-and the adult had been her substitute science teacher for Mr. Telmer. She didn't remember what the students had called her. What was she doing here?

That she knew of, only she and Holly were familiar with the mark and powers. Could it be? Could everyone in this room have the mark and powers too? Had everybody in here been compelled to this room, too?

"Oh, Audrey, come on over!" Holly exclaimed after looking towards the open doorway where Audrey stood.

"O-o-ok," Audrey gulped, slightly intimidated by the others. She quietly and gingerly closed the door and rushed quickly to the group of people, curious about the conversation between them all.

"What's happening?" Audrey quietly queried, looking from one person to the next, still completely astonished that all these people were in this room, the door marked with the symbol on her wrist.

"Apparently, we all have powers and the trident-inside-a-hexagon mark" Audrey's substitute teacher explained with a smile. "You can just call me Meri." Audrey nodded in response. How was it that all of these people, all quite familiar to her, have powers? Wouldn't Audrey have noticed? Well... She guessed not. Why did they have the same mark? That didn't make much sense to her at all.

She then glanced down at her wrist and stifled a scream. Her mark... it was moving. Well, it wasn't moving quickly, it was shifting slowly. The lines went to squiggles, curves, zigzags, and changed randomly. The lines wiggled like snakes and moved around in different alignments. What was happening? Why was her mark moving like that?

Seeing Audrey's widened eyes, Holly showed Audrey her own wrist, her own mark delicately moving too, and began to speak in a reassuring voice. "It's ok, Audrey. It's happening to all of us, too. We were just talking about what it could mean."

With a quivering breath, Audrey bobbed her head and stepped closer to everyone, her mark *moving* even more quickly than before. What is with the mark, and everybody else's? Marks on skin shouldn't move! They're supposed to be still!

"First, we should explain **something** to Audrey. We've been here for a while, taking everything in, and attempting to explain everything," someone Audrey recognized as Adam spoke out.

"Sounds good to me," Meri began, her tone sounding more explanatory as she continued to speak. "So, we all began to

193

come in here, one by one, since we all recognized the symbol on the door."

"I put the symbol on the door," volunteered someone else Audrey recognized as Matt.

"Thank you, Matt," Meri replied with a sarcastic tone. "Now let me continue. As more people came in, more questions were asked, and some were answered."

"We all found out each of us has been pursued by some one person from The Agency," someone Audrey didn't recognize spoke out with a small smile. "I'm Poppy, by the way," she said. "I'm new here." Meri narrowed her eyes at Poppy in frustration, since Poppy had interrupted her, but gave up when Poppy didn't react.

"I was attacked by an agent, too," Audrey stated, raising her hand a little bit.

"That was our assumption," Meri mentioned, clasping her hands together.

Becoming a little more confident with the group, Audrey questioned, "Are we going to do anything about The Agency?"

"Well… since we were all attacked, and it's going to be very unlikely that they're going to give up just like that, we should probably try to find a way to get The Agency to leave us alone," Adam answered with a nod. "But we don't even know where, or what to do."

"I have an idea!" Holly exclaimed, wildly waving her hand in the air. Everybody then turned to her with questioning gazes, including Audrey. "Maybe it could be a blueprint for a weapon! The marks, I mean. Maybe that's why they're moving." Audrey put her finger to her bottom lip and nodded her head in agreement. It made sense to her. It very well could be. It'd be very useful to all of them, especially if they would be dealing with people even more arduous to fight against than Dr. Rhemont.

"No, I don't think that's it," Matt disagreed, shaking his head no. "Though, I do think you're right about our marks having something to do with The Agency."

Everybody briefly nodded and they all began to rub their chins in silent concentration. What could it be? If it possibly can't be blueprints for a weapon, what else could marks do to help with The Agency? Audrey desperately searched her mind to find one idea-even the most stupid idea-but her mind was empty. Why couldn't she think of something? She scrunched up her face, hoping that that could generate more ideas. However, it didn't work.

Well, it's a sure good thing there is a group of people here to think up ideas. They would probably all be much better ideas than the ones I would come up with.

"Could it be a map to get to The Agency?" Holly asked, her orange curls dancing softly as she turned her head. Silence. There was complete silence as Holly looked over all of them. Now that really did make sense! Audrey wasn't just saying that because she was her friend, but because it made sense!

As nobody protested, Audrey was the first to nod, to support her friend. Then, slowly, everyone else began to nod.

"Let's put all of our wrists together," Audrey directed, trying not to sound bossy.

Everybody began to form a circle and put their wrists in the middle.

Audrey glanced to her left to see Holly, and to her right to see Poppy. She then looked at the middle at all of their wrists, and saw that the marks were rapidly changing (which still freaked her out), but as the marks shifted, they were starting to take a better form.

Finally, the lines stopped moving, and it indeed looked like a map, except… it didn't look complete. Why didn't it seem complete? Didn't they have everybody present? Was this not going to work? Were they all doomed to the fear of never knowing when The Agency would strike out at them?

"What are we going to do?" Audrey questioned meekly, staring intently at her wrist, alongside everyone else's.

"I think I know," Holly simply replied, wide-eyed and staring off into space. Everyone turned to face Holly, curious as to what Holly's new genius idea was.

"I know of another gifted child…she lives in another time though. Here, I'll go get her." Holly disappeared.

Images flashed in Holly's mind. She saw a girl with blonde hair and blue eyes. New England. Village. 1700's. Holly knew she needed to go and bring the girl to the room at school with the mark, but she didn't know why. It just seemed like something logical. It was as though this girl from the past was somehow important to the mark. Holly closed her eyes to travel back to an English village in the 1700's. She wasn't entirely sure why she was doing this but she did know something, a girl's name, Wren.

Holly felt the ground under her feet. This trip was quicker than the last trips-even the one to rob the watch shop. Her green eyes opened quickly. She smiled looking out into the village. The rich houses were more clustered in the middle; the smaller houses - she would have called them shacks - were more spread out and farther from the town. She headed to one of the poorer looking shacks. Inside was a girl with blonde hair. Her back was turned towards Holly, hiding her face. Holly smiled lightly to herself. Success, she thought.

"Hello," Holly began, speaking through the open window. "My name is Holly and I-." The figure turned around abruptly, not the same girl, but an entirely enraged one. Spittle flew from her lips as she yelled an unintelligible response. Turning away from her, Holly sprinted back around where she had come from. The old woman hobbled towards her. She felt her gaining slowly. Holly's heart was thudding in her chest-threatening to escape. She ducked around a corner and nearly crashed into a girl with blonde hair and blue eyes who fit the images in Holly's head. Wren. She stared at Holly open-mouthed. Holly extended her hand.
"Come with me," Holly told her. The girl stared at Holly.

"Why are you here? Who are you?" she asked.

"My name is Holly Morrow. I am not from here as you can probably tell," Holly paused as the girl nodded earnestly. "I come from a magical place called the twenty-first century."

"I am Wren," the girl mouthed shakily.

197

The old woman who was chasing Holly rounded the corner shouting something comprehensible this time, "Witch-witches!"

"If you are going to come with me, Wren, by all means-please do hurry up."

"I-" she hesitated, the old woman drawing closer. "How do I know I can trust you?"

"Because of this mark," Holly rolled up her sleeve to show the girl the trident in the hexagon.
The girl's eyes widened, and then she showed Holly her own mark. It was identical. It was as though a magnet was pulling the marks together. Something was missing- the other marks of those who were waiting in the room in the school in the future.

"I will come," the girl said quickly, catching Holly's hand.

The old woman cackled, "Witches." Holly time traveled back to the classroom as the woman's hand came down on the spot where Wren and the girl had been standing. The Agency flashed in Holly's mind, and she gritted her teeth. They would pay for trying to hunt Holly down and turning her friends against her! The solution to their defeat was in the classroom- Holly knew that much.

Once Holly and Wren had entered the room, Poppy brought out a picture of an island. The island looked tropical, and blossoming flowers surrounded a hexagonal concrete building. In the corner there was an outcropping of land and a cliff past a wide stretch of blue that separated it from the island. The stretch of blue that was the ocean had wide, crashing waves. Jack squinted at the photo.

The cliff seems like a good place to land until we can scout out the island.

Josh faded away, drawing himself closer and closer to the cliff in the photo, taking the others in the group with him. Matt remembered the first time Josh had teleported with him, so he put his hand on Josh's arm to keep from being lost in the transaction. The others followed Matt's lead and gripped Josh's arms, too. The classroom faded away from them as the smell of salt and the sound of rushing waves grew stronger. They had arrived. They were on the cliff. They were in the place in the photograph.

Lily

We started to walk to the raft. Everyone climbed into the raft except for me. I would pull the boat in the water while navigating. Once everyone was in the raft, I took a head count. It was very important, especially with the preciseness of the plan we had thought up, to have everyone present. After the head count was over, I jumped into the frigid water. The lifeless water was plain and dull, but the appearance of the water was the least of my concerns. Two of the people on the boat started to paddle. My job was to navigate and pull the boat if needed, for the boat only came with two paddles. Seconds turned into minutes, and minutes turned into hours, but we were still far from the island. We had several short conversations, but other than that, not much really happened on the journey to the island. I didn't blame the others for being quiet; they were all probably thinking about the same thing- whether or not they would make it out alive. We were just far away enough to see the curve of the island, and to distinguish the various shades of green in the trees. The water was very lifeless with only a couple of small white fish here and there. It was ninety five degrees out, and everyone was very hot because the sky was empty except for a couple of almost transparent clouds.
After what seemed like hours, we could make out the island a little clearer. Even though we were still about an hour away, the view gave us hope to carry on. The island got bigger and bigger until I could see the hot sand blowing in the wind. I noticed that the water looked more tropical and

colorful than before. Colorful fish of various sizes carelessly swam around in the transparent and light blue water. As we got closer to the island, I noticed something round and orange. After getting a little closer to the mysterious object, I saw that it had millions of little almost string-like legs below it. After thinking about it, I realized that only one sea creature could look like this. It was the Lion's Mane jellyfish. I couldn't turn back though, because we all had to take risks to follow through with the plan. I kept going.

Finally we got to the island. We all helped hide the raft in some bushes and approached the building.

Holly stood on the beach, shaking wet droplets from her hair and clothes. The building in front of the group seemed to loom, shadowing the newcomers beneath its bulky cement structure. The group was small, but determined all the same. Holly and the others trudged up the sandy slope. Holly ran her fingers along the sides of the cement complex expanding before her, searching for an entrance. Rounding a corner, she noticed a door in front of them. It was quite plain and inconspicuous, blending in with the rough cement of the wall.

Audrey laughed as her wet sneakers squelched against the rocks of the beach. Alfred pushed Lily teasingly.
"Why'd you have to get us all wet? What was that for? I mean, seriously…couldn't you have given us a dry ride?"
"Sorry. Not my fault."
Matt stared up at the huge grey building rising up in front of them. The Bermuda Triangle was not a triangle. It was a hexagon. Well, the building was. It looked just like The Mark.
"Hey, Matt! Get over here!" shouted Adam. He had his hands on a magnificent door. "It's your turn. Go in there and unlock it."
"Anything to get us closer to defeating the Agency." Matt responded, filled with hatred for the group that hunted down super-humans to study them or lock them away.
The large metal door covered in dials, locks, bolts, and handles began to blur as he walked closer and closer and

then, it was gone. He had gone through it. Matt looked for a handle. None. All that was there was a small lock. Locked on both sides?

Hmm… *Perhaps I could look inside of the door itself?* He thought. Inside he went. He saw gears and pulleys and axels. There were tumblers and well.

Matt counted thirty four of them, far more than the normal lock, which had two of three. This was the most complicated lock he had ever seen.

He saw two rods connecting to where the locks were on the outside. He experimentally turned the rod. A whole line of gears and axels rotated in the door but stopped near the top. A gear was slightly separated from another, but as it turned, it got closer, but sadly, not close enough. He turned the other rod, and the same thing happened.

"Oh, how did I not realize that?" Matt slapped his forehead at his stupidity. He turned both rods at the same time and the gears connected. The metal shell of the door revealed an etching of a circle that slipped into a slot in the door. The gears collapsed to make a clear path through the door. Now it was open, but was it safe to go in?

Matt called to the rest of the group.

"Hey, guys! It's open!"

They tiptoed single file into the narrow marble hallway. The walls were decorated with silver plaques and fancy awards.

"Why are we tiptoeing?" Wren asked Holly.

"We don't want *them* to hear us. It's supposed to be a surprise attack," she answered. After a few minutes passing in this manner, Adam, who was at the front of the pack,

stopped suddenly. Everyone froze and craned their necks to see what had halted their mission. Adam filled them in. "There's a hallway jutting out from this one. It's wider. Should we take it, or keep going?" he asked the group. Poppy answered immediately. "Take it."
"How do you know?" Meri inquired.
Poppy tensed. "Believe me, you should take it. I have a feeling this will lead us exactly where we need to go."
"Okay," Adam agreed. "If you're certain."
They continued on. Adam stopped again. "There's another hallway on the right, and a door on the left. Any ideas?"
"Definitely left," Poppy exclaimed.

Everyone stopped dead in their tracks as soon as gentle footsteps came their way.
"Oh great," Holly muttered with a slight groan.
Audrey's hand instantly went to her neck and Audrey felt her fire pendant necklace. Audrey's father still had not made her ice pendant necklace, but she would manage. Her flames would probably be enough.
Audrey stared down the hallway and allowed a large, warm fire to flicker calmly above the palm of her hand. Four people strolled calmly down the hall, straight towards Audrey and her friends. They all held handcuffs and pistols. Audrey looked over the people quickly and instantly saw a recognizable face. Her jaw dropped to the ground and her pupils expanded in shock.
"What's wrong, Audrey?" Holly questioned, looking at her surprised face.
"Oh my…. gosh," Audrey whispered. The person so recognizable was a woman with blond hair and hazel eyes,

boldly smirking at Audrey and everyone else. Dr. Rhemont. Again. Oh no…

The other three people, however, didn't seem familiar to her at all. There were two men and a woman. Both of the men were tall, muscular in a scary way and had deep blue eyes. One of the men had gray hair, while the other man had light brown hair. The woman looked like she was in her early sixties at a closer glance, and had white streaks in her blonde hair that fell over her chestnut eyes.

"Oh, it's all the young super kinetic anomalies," Dr. Rhemont snickered, twisting a key to unlock the handcuffs she had and loading the pistol with a quick click. "We've been waiting to see you all. It's such a pleasure for us!" Audrey's flame burned brighter with her quiet rage.

Then, as they continued walking, Dr. Rhemont's gaze turned to Audrey's flame. "It's so lovely to see you, Audrey!" Dr. Rhemont trilled. "The last time we bumped into one another, you were quite *icy* towards me." Dr. Rhemont laughed at her own joke, and her companions chuckled along too.

"What do you want?" Poppy challenged.

"All of you," the other woman responded with a hiss. "Right, Dr. Rhemont?" And the woman got a brief nod in return from Dr. Rhemont.

Dr. Rhemont and her group were just a few feet away from Audrey.

Why hadn't we spent that time escaping or fighting? Why hadn't I done anything? Audrey thought frantically.

Well, since Dr. Rhemont has her fire-resistant lotion, I'll have to go after her three vulnerable companions.

Audrey instantly made her flames swirl forward and poked and prodded at her companions, just to scare them away, because she didn't want anybody to be badly hurt. Audrey extinguished her roaring fire and glanced at Dr. Rhemont's companions. But there they stood all happy and cruel, and guess what, they weren't even singed. Audrey guessed that Dr. Rhemont shared her fire-resistant lotion. Wonderful. Just wonderful.

"Oh, yeah, I forgot to tell you, we go to the same supermarket, and they decided they wanted some lotion, too," Dr. Rhemont chortled. She and her companions were now standing right in front of us. Dr. Rhemont's stale breath hit Audrey as she inhaled and exhaled with the most wild grin. "I've got something for all of your friends, but don't worry, we've got something for you, too." Then, at the same time, they all held up their handcuffs, the silver shining brightly despite the lack of light.

Before the children with powers could even move a muscle, Dr. Rhemont and her cruel helpers all grabbed two or three of the people with powers and quickly put their hands behind their backs to cuff them. And, of course, Dr. Rhemont got Audrey, and Audrey could tell she was enjoying every moment. Then they began walking Audrey away, with what seemed to be a certain sense of where to go.

As they walked, Dr. Rhemont happily spoke. "Now, these handcuffs aren't just ordinary handcuffs. These were all suited for each of you when we began to make them."

"Tell them about the handcuffs, Clementine!" urged the young man. "So they know that **we're** just as able to defend ourselves as they can!"

208

"I was going to, dimwit! Just be quiet!" Dr. Rhemont hissed and abruptly stopped, along with her companions, jerking everyone into a quiet stop. "I do the talking here."

"Yes, doctor," the young man muttered sadly. Audrey almost felt kind of bad for him. She would completely feel bad for him, but then he did have her friends cuffed. The "doctor" led them to a holding place.

Dr. Rhemont continued walking, which was the cue for her companions to begin walking, too. "Well, you see, we engineered these handcuffs and specialized them for each and every one of you. We put magnets to keep the atoms balanced so the one who can walk through walls currently can't. There is one handcuff that keeps the person from shifting through time --- it's too complicated to explain. One to keep one of you from flying, one for keeping one of you from using telekinesis, and one for each of the other super kinetic anomalies. That reminds me..." Dr. Rhemont then reached for Audrey's neck, snatched her necklace, snapped it off, and stuffed it into her gun holster. *Her necklace! How dare she! My flames are the only thing I could control!* "We're almost to your comfy little holding cell!"

Up ahead, a barred area formed a small cell with what looked like a small bench inside. A guard waited at the door, and held what seemed to be keys, and he also held a gun, but it wasn't a pistol. I don't really know the different guns, all I knew was that his gun was much larger than Dr. Rhemont's and her companion's small guns.

"Open the door," the older man ordered with a raspy voice. "We have **them**."

The guard nodded, unlocked the door, and opened the door, signaling for Dr. Rhemont and her companions to shove them into the little cell.

They began to shove them in, first taking off handcuffs, except for Matt's of course, and Dr. Rhemont got the courtesy of shoving Audrey into the cell, just like she had with Rosemary at the hospital.

The door then slid shut, trapping everyone inside the cell, which was not suitable for eleven people.

"Have fun! But, don't worry, someone'll be coming to get you later. In a few hours about," Dr. Rhemont laughed cheerfully, and snuck off to who knew where with her companions.

She locked us all in this tiny little cell! And she took the necklace! How was Audrey supposed to use her powers to help now?

Audrey gritted her teeth and grasped the bars with fiery warm hands. The bar hadn't melted, no matter how much she willed for it too.

Stop, she told her fire, *stop*. Audrey's hands slowly cooled and the bars were no longer being heated.

Ignite, she told her fire, and guess what, her fire ignited.

I guess I don't need the necklace to control my flames. Hopefully it would work with my ice, too.

Audrey's hands fizzled out. It was a good idea, Lily thought. Too bad it didn't work. Holly slumped against the wall and sighed. She was tired. Really tired. They weren't done yet, though. They were stuck in a cell in the middle of The Agency building. They were very far from finished. Wren scooted over to Holly.

210

"What do you think they'll do to us?" She asked.

"I don't know. It doesn't matter, though. We'll be long gone before they get back."

"How do you know?"

"I can time travel. I know."

"Oh, I forgot about that. So, how do we do it?"

"Do what?"

"You know, finish off The Agency."

"I didn't actually check. I had a problem once when I tried to meet my future self. Some time paradox thing. I was forced to leave immediately."

"Oh…but you mean you saw yourself?!"

"Yup. I was pretty old. Ninety two maybe."

"So, you're sure you're going to survive, then?"

"Oh, yeah I guess I will. I wish I could tell you if you will, I'm sorry."

"Its okay… I'm not sure I would want to know."

Poppy stood stiffly against the cell wall. She stared into space as Meri yawned and stretched next to her. Audrey pressed her cheek against the bars and recoiled. They were burning hot.

"Ow!" she yelped.

"I have an idea," said Adam.

Mia looked outside the prison cell, trying to spot a key. Her eyes flitted back and forth, until boom! She saw the key. It was hanging over a big metal desk. She had her eyes glued onto the keys as she grasped the cold prison bars. She closed her eyes and took a deep breath. Soon she could feel herself morphing. She opened her eyes, and was shocked at what she saw. She saw three hundred different fragments of the room, from all different directions. She must have fallen over because she was very close to the floor, looking up at her friends. What?! This was confusing. Mia stumbled over as she got up and rushed this way and that.

"Ants!" Poppy exclaimed, pointing down at where Mia felt herself to be.

I'm ants?! Mia thought.

She looked through the crack below the prison cell. She then used her new bodies to scurry through the cell and towards the key. She knew if she could get the key, she could carry it on her many backs and scurry back to the cell to everyone else. But the prison guard had the key… She slowly crept up on the prison cell guard, and soon she was all over his legs. She felt his skin grow burning hot as she bit hard with her razor-sharp pinchers into his weak flesh.

This is so easy! Is this really all it will take? A few bites from my poisonous jaws?

The guard screamed in pain. She kept biting him. As the minutes passed, his skin grew colder, and his screams turned to whimpers. Finally, his head rolled back, and he rolled from his chair onto the cement floor.

Good work colony! She thought proudly to herself.

She quickly climbed into his pocket and grabbed the key. She glanced back to see his poisoned, lifeless body lying on the floor. Cold sweats rolled from his forehead and onto his cracking lips, forever open in a silent gasp. She had done what she had to do, and now, thankfully, it was done.

The kids unlocked the door and ran from the cell, out the door, and into a courtyard. Alfred looked at his surroundings. He was in a lone courtyard surrounded by trees and various shrubs. It was then that he realized Wren was with him, and knew what he needed to do. He quickly scurried over to one of the trees and made it bigger. The group followed his lead, and quickly made the trees into animate objects. This went on until all of the trees were large, animate objects. This made up a small army, all of the trees together. They were a formidable opponent to any foe. The problem was that they made a lot of noise and that they would soon scare people out of the building. There were a few people who had no problem with the trees, however. Soon, many people stepped out of the building to join the fight.

Wren had animated the trees and the vines had roped around the agent's wrists.

The agents were struggling against the vines wildly. It would be difficult for them to get out of that mess, but they could get out eventually, and then **that** would not be good. So that needed to be fixed.

Audrey summoned her ice with some difficulty, which was not as difficult as she assumed it would've been, and looked to her right hand.

A semi-solid ball of ice floated above her hand, and she concentrated on that ball of ice so it would stay at her command and wouldn't go crazy. Her hand trembled furiously at the complete concentration she had to use just with that ball of semi-solid ice.

The agents were struggling so much that they hadn't even realized the ice that floated above her hand. Well, they'd find out soon.

She closed her eyes and imagined where she wanted her ice to go. She focused on her ice for just a second, and then allowed it to shoot forwards, becoming fully solid as it traveled through the air.

A few screams of pain pierced the air and her eyes opened immediately. Had she injured somebody horribly?

Audrey glanced over to the agents, faces contorted in horror as they looked at their wrists. Their wrists... they had the vines wrapped around them, and a big, solid chunk of ice coated the vines and the remaining part of their wrists. So, she guessed she hadn't injured them too badly then... Oh well.

There's no time to stop and think about it anyways. Everybody must have thought the same thing, because they all began to run down the courtyard, pushing the trapped agents out of mind, and heading to the next stage of bad guy central.

All of them were panting, as the confused shouts of men echoed through the newly grown trees. In front of them, a large, yawning doorway sprung out of the thick, dark walls. Left with no choice, as the trees had grown all the way around them, they slowly, warily crossed over the threshold. Meri began breathing hard, as her experiences in dark places began to affect her. She held out her hand, and a torch popped into it. Open-mouthed she stared at it. "I asked for a flashlight," she said. With the torchlight flickering on the walls, they continued to edge forward, not knowing what to expect. They walked through another doorway, and as they walked in, a series of halogen lights flashed on above them. They were in a large room; it looked as if multiple football fields could fit inside. There were three men in suits standing calmly, looking at the youths. Backing them were six soldiers, holding rifles, and dressed in Tactical Armor. The group backed up and realized- what could they do, the nine of them against us? Smith began talking in his baritone, "Give up, or you will perish." Defiantly, they stood there quietly, not uttering a word. Telmer said, "Very well." John Doe immediately began to shimmer. Then, another John Doe stepped out of his body, and another out of each copy. He did this until there were 64 of him. Telmer stepped forward, flames alight in his eyes. Evans just stood there smugly, looking as though he were invincible.

Each one took a deep breath and they all faded in and out, and then appeared in a ring around everyone, spaced out so that they were around an arm's length apart.

Telmer stated, "Don't do this please. I don't want to hurt you."

In response, Adam reached his hand out, flung one of the mercenaries into the window and sneered at him, "What will you do?"

"This," he clapped his hands together, and instead of a clap, a massive wave of the thunder echoed around the room. Everyone fell to their knees. However, all of his allies were groaning as well. Poppy was able to float into the air, dart forward, and hit Telmer. Sent reeling, the continuous echoing sound stopped. He looked up, in anger, and he looked to Doe. Three of his clones rushed after her. Adam slammed one of them down, and it faded into nothing. He began to bat the clones aside, but every time one went down, another stepped out of a clone. Audrey began to throw fire at Telmer. However, every time a ball left her hand, it was absorbed. Alfred ran up to Evan and put his hand on Evan's arm. Alfred concentrated and tried to make him younger, but Evans glowed blue and nothing happened. Evan brought his fist around and lifted Alfred off the ground with a devastating blow. All the while the soldiers were firing. One of them accidentally shot Telmer in the leg. He turned around, and let loose a massive ball of fire at the soldier, actually melting him. Telmer touched his wound, and it actually faded off of his skin. Shaking himself John stood up. He began to fade from sight. He appeared behind Audrey and clipped her. At the contact she recoiled, and sent an ice burst at him. It covered his features, and slowly spread over his body. It covered his head and froze him in place. There were now three soldiers left and what was now The Two. David ran forward and grabbed Evans, but instead of throwing him, his arm, kind of deflated, and a bullet ran through his chest. He fell to the ground, lifeless. Devastated, Adam fell to his knees and let loose a huge telekinetic blast, throwing everyone to the walls, including his friends. However, Evans stood unruffled. The three soldiers were killed and Telmer hit hard. Audrey was lying on the ground near Evans, and half unconscious. Ice began to spread out from her body, and without him noticing, it climbed up his legs. He tried to walk, and found that he couldn't. Thrashing in panic, he struggled as the ice climbed over his head, and covered him. Now there was one left. Mr. Telmer. He ran forward and grabbed Audrey's neck. Struggling, she loosed fire at him. The flames disappeared. Everyone in the room ran at him, even Sasha, but he was fast enough, that he electrocuted everyone in the room but Audrey. At that moment, ice began to spread up his arm.

The whole room was just chaotic. There were a few agents battling those with powers on the good side.

There was kicking, hitting, biting and spitting. Electricity crackled throughout the room, and many people took different forms. Random objects were lifted in the air from telekinesis and flew through the air, and the ground beneath her feet didn't feel as stable as it had before. There were sixty-four copies of a man with brown hair and brown eyes and the room felt hot from all of the crackling energy. It wasn't very lovely.

Audrey got a quick glimpse of Holly, and she saw from the torso up, Holly had disappeared, only to return quickly, with a long, shining silver sword in hand that seemed to have come from medieval times.

Audrey was the only one without an opponent. *Where's somebody that I can battle?* She thought. *I mean, I can't leave here without battling someone, right?* Audrey didn't care if she hurt anybody now. She just wanted to fight! If she didn't get to have an epic battle, she literally would attack a bush!

Then, a tall shadow loomed over her. She spun around and cowered at the menacing figure. The person had one blue eye and one green eye, and he had slick black hair. He had a soul patch on his chin, and was incredibly tall. *Mr. Telmer? My science teacher? What was he doing here? Was he an agent?* And next to him were two other people she didn't recognize.

"Oh hello, Audrey," Mr. Telmer chuckled. "Now this will be fun."

How am I supposed to fight my teacher? I could get a detention for that! Audrey thought.

"Well, come on Audrey, use your fire on me!" Mr. Telmer taunted, sneering cruelly at her. "Unless you're too weak." *Weak?!? Did he just call me weak?!?*

*He's asking for it. Detention or no detention, he's on the bad side **and** he called me weak! Teachers aren't supposed to do that!* An inferno inside of Audrey lit up as she started her own flame flickering wildly.

At least I get my battle now! I won't have to attack a bush anymore! All bushes are now safe!

She then pulled herself back to reality and unleashed a massive wave of embers and pushed that colossal wave of embers to Mr. Telmer, feeling a bit too confident with herself.

Her flames went towards Mr. Telmer but they didn't scorch him. Her flames had actually disappeared before they had come even a foot in front of Mr. Telmer.

That wasn't her intended purpose though. Her flames should've at least reached behind him. They shouldn't have disappeared without a trace of smoke! *What happened?*

"Dumbfounded?" Mr. Telmer questioned with a deep laugh. Audrey's only response was her dropped jaw and silence. Would he explain what had happened like Dr. Rhemont had done?

Mr. Telmer then shot a massive wave of flames at her, and Audrey had barely gotten out of the fire's path. The fire still had gotten her, and it hurt. She glanced down at her left arm and saw raw, burnt, blistered skin where Mr. Telmer had burnt her.

Just looking at her burnt wound made her wince and tense up. *I'm going to need to be bandaged up, but obviously now isn't the time to deal with the situation.*

I guess Mr. Telmer is much smarter than Dr. Rhemont, he hadn't explained anything, and he just went in for an attack. It also seemed that Mr. Telmer had powers too. Power over flames, she presumed. She didn't really know. She kind of doubted it.

But everyone else was occupied. All of the agents were much stronger and smarter than Audrey had expected them to be. *This was much more difficult than expected, but we have to defeat The Agency, however, in order for that to happen, we have to pull through.*

She turned her attention back to her conniving opponent, Mr. Telmer, and summoned another ball of fire swiftly and at ease, holding the blaze back and allowing the blaze to build up, holding the massive ball of fire with her hand.

Maybe if she sent her fire at him faster, then she could slip past Mr. Telmer's defenses. It did seem logical.

She flicked her wrist quickly and saw her flames going faster than she had ever sent them before. Hopefully it would work this time.

However, it didn't. Again, her flames completely disappeared just a foot in front of Mr. Telmer.

Seriously, what was happening to her flames? Were her flames faulty? No, it couldn't be.

Mr. Telmer then sent flames right back at her, and she wasn't fast enough this time. The embers had engulfed her whole right leg, leaving her right leg raw, burnt and in complete pain.

Audrey grunted and collapsed, her leg in too much agony to support the rest of her. Tears welled in her eyes and they slid down her face, the pain of her arm contributing to the searing pain in her leg. Her whole leg tingled as she gaped at her wound. She attempted to push her jeans up so she could see her ankle, but her raw skin was stuck to the fabric like glue to paper, and that sent only a worse burning pain throughout her whole body. *How could Mr. Telmer do that? Teachers shouldn't burn their students! That really needs to be an official rule.*

How am I supposed to fight Mr. Telmer now in my condition? I'm in too much pain! I could die! Yeah, some of the pain has ebbed away, but my leg still burns like a thousand suns.

A coolness flowed through her, and Audrey saw, out of the corner of her eye, that ice, coming from her, went towards the two men who had been at Mr. Telmer's side. Ice began to crawl up their ankles and they were both soon covered with ice.

The tall shadow again loomed over her. She saw Mr. Telmer's hand going to her throat. He picked her up by the throat and lifted her high into the air, his nails digging into her neck, and her right leg hanging limply.

"Put me... down!" Audrey demanded with a hoarse voice, struggling for air.

"No little one. All of you super kinetic anomalies need to be taken care of," Mr. Telmer whispered, his grip on her neck tightening. She couldn't breathe. She couldn't concentrate no matter how much she wanted to-how much she needed to. *I can't die! I need to go home, home to my mom, dad and sister, Rosemary.* But there was nothing she

226

could do, and the edges of her vision were becoming pitch black, and the pain was becoming even angrier, as it ripped through her burnt flesh. *Was this how it felt to die?* Mr. Telmer then put his head next to her, and whispered, "I have the power to absorb energy and pain. I am also immortal, and sadly, it seems it is time for the fire to flicker one last time and go out forever."

Audrey anxiously ripped and tore at the large hands holding her up by the neck and tried to cough. Everything was beginning to turn black as she tried to breathe in, but no air would come in, and she was becoming extremely dizzy.

Then a voice called out, "Freeze him, Audrey! Ice has no energy, so he can't absorb the ice!"

Audrey closed her eyes and focused on what energy she had left inside of her to summon her ice and freeze Mr. Telmer, thankful for whoever had yelled out to her.

Ice crackled and the grip around her neck softened. She tore wildly again at the stubborn fingers and pried them off, instantly falling to the hard ground, but she was unharmed. She took in a few deep quick breaths and the black at the edges of her vision disappeared slowly. She could breathe. Air had never tasted sweeter in her whole life before. And her leg and arm no longer hurt. Mr. Telmer must've forcefully absorbed her pain as she had frozen him.

Oh, yes, she had frozen him! She had almost forgotten about that! Still lying on the ground, she turned to face Mr. Telmer and her eyes nearly popped out of their sockets. Mr. Telmer was covered in a thick coating of ice with his right arm stretched out to the side, and he looked like he was inside an ice cube. His face was contorted in complete horror, and the ice around him looked opaque and foggy. Only his one hand wasn't covered in ice. That was the hand that he had been choking her with. She instantly shot ice at his hand and he was covered up completely.

We had done it! I mean, there was probably more to do to take care of everything, but we had done it! Telmer, and the other two, whom she didn't know the names of, were taken care of.

Audrey looked out into the chaos again and glanced back at Mr. Telmer, his arm outstretched, and smiled. Another pest had been taken care of by being encased in ice.

When the battle was done, the long and tedious process of flying and teleporting everyone off the island had begun. Soon only Holly was left. "Come back soon!" Holly called to Poppy's disappearing form. The battle had ended when Audrey had frozen Mr. Telmer. Here Holly was on a deserted island in the Bermuda Triangle, sitting on the beach. A rustling noise in the bush caught her attention. She stood up, brushing the sand from her jeans. Of all the people she thought she would see, Lauren was the last person she expected. But there Lauren was, dragging herself through the undergrowth. "You're alive?" Holly's wonder had stolen her breath.

Lauren did the most incredible thing- she laughed. She stared back to the demolished headquarters of The Agency.

"It was never really supposed to be like this," Lauren murmured softly. Holly plunked down next to her.

"What are you saying?"

"What I'm saying is there was an argument involving the Laurelly's and the leaders of The Agency before it really was The Agency. There were half-finished plans to form an academy. A school, mean to train, not to hurt," Lauren explained.

"And now what are we supposed to do?" Holly pondered hesitantly. She smiled a little.

"Isn't it obvious- we create The Academy."

I waited near the beautiful entryway to my favorite place on Earth, The Academy. Audrey's parents had great ideas for the newly managed Agency. After Telmer was defeated, they had taken over, and it became The Academy, a school and training center for people with superhuman powers.

I was waiting because we had recently admitted a new student to the school. I was assigned to give the new student a tour because I was one of the superhuman mentors.

"Are you Casey?" I asked a young boy who had just stepped out of a helicopter near the entryway. He was tall, with dark brown hair and green eyes.

"Yes, are you my mentor?" Casey wondered.

"I am one of them, and call me Matt," I responded. "Today I'll show you around school."

We passed by a classroom full of noisy children and reached an empty one. The sign by the door read: "Room 104, Prof. Caldwell."

"This is Professor Caldwell's room. He teaches science. Science is very important here at The Academy." I told Casey. We moved toward the office. "The leaders of this school are the parents of Audrey, who is one of your other mentors."

"Who is that? He seems kind of scary." Casey pointed to a bulky kid with bright blond hair. He wore a football jacket.

"Oh, him? Don't worry, he's not scary. His name is Stewart, but he goes by Shocky. He's one of my close friends." I said.

"Why do you call him Shocky?" Casey asked in a whisper.

"Well, it was originally because of his last name, Shockler, but now everybody calls him that because of his special powers. He can use stray static electricity in the air to shock things." I answered. "He acquired the powers after being tased seven times in the chest."

"There are a lot of adult students here." Casey reported. "Why is that?"

"One of our mentors traveled through a time rift and retrieved super humans from an Old English insane asylum. Our school nurse, Dr. Rhemont, explained the situation to them. At first, they went a little crazy, but luckily, she was able to calm them down and explain where they were. Now, they are students here at The Academy." I continued walking further, nearing the end of the hall. This was the best part of the tour.

"Alright, this is the end of the tour." I gestured towards a large block of ice at the end of the hall.

"What is it?" Casey asked, dumbfounded.

"That," I stated, "is the best maximum security prison on Earth. It contains a very evil man named Dr. Telmer."

"How'd he get in there?" Casey wondered.

"How about I start from the very beginning?"

237

This book was planned, written and edited by the 7th and 8th grade students of Mimmi Beck's writing club 2015.

Questions or comments? Email: mimmib@aol.com

43900285R00138